MR. NOVEMBER

Calendar Boys Series

NICOLE S. GOODIN

Mr. November
Published by Nicole S. Goodin
ISBN: 978-0-9951276-5-4
Copyright 2019 by Nicole S. Goodin
All rights reserved. ©
First published November 2019

Cover design by Nicole Goodin
Images purchased from Shutterstock
Editing by Spell Bound

For all the babes born in November

CHAPTER ONE

Rhett

I scan the beach and out into the water beyond, looking for any signs of distress from the hundreds of beach goers out making the most of the scorching heat.

I scowl as my gaze catches on the news crew further down the sand. I don't have a problem with their reporting, but live TV turns people stupid, and with the heavy sets rolling in today, stupid isn't what I'm hoping for.

I radio down to Nick; he and Becca are patrolling the east side of the beach, and Georgie and I have the west.

"Can you two come our way a bit? We've got a camera crew down here and I'm going to go down and make sure no one does anything dumb."

The radio crackles and then Nick replies. "Copy that, boss, we'll close the gap."

I clip it back on the band of my shorts and jog the short distance to Georgie. "I'm going to go keep an eye on things down there. You good up here?"

She nods. "I've got this, just make sure we don't have a repeat of last time." She scowls at the reporter.

I know exactly what she's referring to.

I shake my head in disbelief. Some people will do anything to get themselves on TV.

Last time it took us half an hour to get the nude surfer out of the water and up onto the beach before the police could take him away.

I'm not against nudist beaches or anything, but this isn't one of them.

The poor kids around were probably scarred for days by the dude's hairy balls.

I head down the beach towards the camera crew to get a better look.

Great.

It's Emily Simons.

She's so hungry for a good story she'd chew her own leg off.

She smiles brightly as she sees me approaching. "Morning, Rhett." She bats her lashes at me.

She's motivated in more ways than one. The woman has been angling for a date for the past six months. I'm starting to think that's why she finds these 'stories' down at my beach so often.

I've spent half of my life down on these shores, first as a kid, then a junior lifeguard, then a senior, and now as the head lifeguard – my job for the past five years.

It's my dream job – the *Baywatch* jokes from my mates aside.

"How are you doing, Emily?"

"Better now." She beams, and I manage to resist the urge to roll my eyes. Just. Only just.

The woman is the epitome of a walking cliché and she doesn't even seem to know it.

"Just thought I'd come down and keep an eye on things, you know... after last time."

"Oh, *sure*." She gives me a smile that gives me the distinct impression that she thinks I'm playing coy – like I'm just looking for an excuse to get closer to her.

She couldn't be further from the truth.

She says something to her camera guy and takes a step in my direction.

Ah crap.

Here we go again.

My radio beeps on my hip, right as I start to scramble for a reason to keep my distance from her.

I shouldn't be grateful for a possible emergency, but I am.

Saved by the bell.

"Boss, we've got a situation out back," Blake – the senior lifeguard in the patrol tower tells me.

I've got the radio in my hand in a flash. "Where?"

"Directly in line with your position, back of the breakers."

I rush to the edge of the water, but I can't see shit from down here, the swell is too big.

"Am I getting wet?" I demand.

"I dunno, boss, she's not got her arm in the air yet, but she's caught in that rip."

"Becca, get down here," I radio over to my team.

Becca might only be a junior, but she could outswim any of us with her eyes shut, and with conditions like this, she'll be valuable.

"On my way," she replies without missing a beat.

"Sorry, boss, no time, you need to get out there, *now*," Blake cuts in, letting me know the situation has escalated. This woman might not have been in trouble before, but she is now.

Shit.

Becca won't be here for a couple of minutes. It can't wait that long.

I drop the radio, drag my shirt over my head, grab the rescue tube from the nearby flag, and plough my way through the shallow water and crashing waves.

I hear Emily yell at her camera crew to start rolling. *Vulture.*

I dive under huge wave after huge wave until I get to the back of the breakers, and *Jesus*, this isn't just a rip, it's the mother of all rips; it's dragging me out to sea.

I saw it earlier, shifted the flags accordingly, but I had no idea it was this powerful or I would have moved every swimmer well clear.

Rips are our biggest problem on this beach.

It doesn't seem to matter how much we educate the public on what to do if they get caught in a rip – ninety percent of the time they'll still try their hardest to swim against it, usually to the point where they're exhausted and near drowning.

I search, looking desperately for the woman. I nearly miss her head bobbing up and down, almost completely under water.

My arms cut through the choppy water and I'm at her side in a few seconds.

"Miss!" I call, but she doesn't respond.

I reach underwater, dragging her face above the surface, but she's not responding – her eyes are closed, and her body is limp.

I strap the tube around her middle and flip her back against my chest, I'm about to start the long swim back to shore when I hear the roar of the rescue boat's engine.

Thank god for that.

Nick spins the boat. Becca is in the front, already leaning over the edge, her arm extended to help me drag the lifeless woman in.

I heave her from the water and throw myself over the side of the pontoon, my body still half in the water when Nick hits the accelerator.

Becca has the tube unclipped and the woman on her back and I'm kneeling next to her, checking for signs of life in the very next second.

We work well together, me and my team, this is what we do.

"She's not breathing."

I know this isn't the time for trivial shit, but this woman, she smells like strawberries and cream – so sweet my mouth is practically watering.

"The ambulance is already on its way, boss," Nick responds.

The engine squeals as we fly down the face of a wave, getting airborne.

I don't know how the hell this woman managed to get all the way out back – I'm the strongest swimmer here – other than Becca, and that was work, even for me.

Nick speeds us towards the shore, the boat skidding to a stop in the wet sand.

"Starting CPR," I announce as soon as we're stationary.

I press my hands to her chest and press down thirty times, her chest jerking with the movement.

"C'mon, baby," I murmur to her.

Two breaths, thirty more compressions.

I can't hear anything but my own breath ringing in my ears.

Breathe, dammit, I beg her silently.

"Ambulance is here," Becca calls out, rushing from the boat to clear a path so the paramedics can get through the hordes of people that have crowded around to get a better view.

I give her chest another heavy thump and water bubbles from her mouth.

"Rhett..." Nick says, seeing it too.

I roll her on her side, and she coughs, more water spilling from her mouth.

She coughs again, her hands flying up to her throat, and I almost cry in relief.

She's alive.

"Easy... *easy*." I soothe her as I roll her over gently and come face to face with the most incredible set of eyes I've ever seen.

Molten gold, burning into mine. "You're going to be alright," I whisper.

CHAPTER TWO

Libby

My head pounds as I try to make sense of the stranger hovering above me and the searing pain in my chest and throat.

"Slow, easy breaths," he says softly, "just nice and easy."

I do what he says and refrain from dragging in deep, gulping breaths like my head is screaming at me to do.

"That's it, you got it, sweetheart," he praises, his brown eyes never leaving mine.

This is clearly not the time, I don't know where I am or what's wrong with me, but it's not lost on me just how beautiful this mystery man is.

"I'm going to sit you up," he says, and I stare at him like a deer in headlights as he slips his hands around my shivering body and lifts me up to a sitting position.

It's only then that I notice we're not alone, and I'm in a boat.

"Hey, you scared us there for a minute," another guy says as he reaches out and drapes a silver blanket over me.

"Where am I?" I ask, but nothing much comes out, just a hoarse whisper.

"You're on the beach," the man with his hands on me replies, drawing my attention back to him. "You got into some trouble in the water. We had to pull you out."

My memory comes back in a rush. "The rip," I rasp.

He nods, his face only inches from mine. "It's a nasty one. You were lucky."

I don't feel very lucky, I feel like I'm on death's door.

I was swimming, just like I do every day, when the current changed and I got pulled out of the flagged area, right towards the huge rip. I tried to fight the current, but I couldn't. I know damn well you're meant to swim with the rip and not against it, but I panicked.

I try to twist and wince in pain.

"Just try and relax," he encourages, pressing his arm to my back, encouraging me to lean back on him, so I do. "I had to do CPR. You could have broken ribs."

CPR... broken ribs?

A tear slips down my cheek.

I nearly died.

"Here they are," he whispers softly in my ear. "They're going to take good care of you."

A chorus of cheers and claps starts, and I look around and see all the people surrounding us. More importantly, all the people staring at *me.*

I shrink back, but the pain in my chest and the arm of whoever this guy is, stop me.

"It's okay," he whispers, but it's *not.* He doesn't get it – some of those people have their phones out, taking photos, videos even... and that's when I see it, the huge TV camera, pointed right in my direction.

I throw myself forward, almost vomiting with the pain. I grit my teeth as the roll of nausea subsides.

"What are you doi–"

"Turn the videos off," I try to yell, but it comes out barely audible.

"Let's just get you in the ambulance," he says, reaching for me.

"No cameras," I hiss, my throat screaming in protest.

Our eyes meet and his bewildered expression would be comical if this wasn't such a fucking disaster.

"How is she, Rhett?" I hear a female voice ask.

Rhett. The name repeats in my head as he speaks. "She's in a lot of pain. At risk of secondary drowning, possible broken ribs – I had to work pretty hard to get her back."

"Miss?" the new voice questions me, but I refuse to look up.

"I don't know what's going on," Rhett tells her, "but she needs medical attention, right now."

"I'm not going until the cameras are gone," I whisper, tears pooling in my eyes.

"No time, I'm afraid," Rhett says, as I feel his arms wrap around me. "You can worry about unflattering photos later."

If only that was all it was, but I don't have a choice.

He lifts me clean off the boat floor, and I'm useless to fight him; I'm in too much pain, I'm too tired. I'm like a dead weight in his arms, but he doesn't seem to notice. He lays me ever so gently on a stretcher and together they carry me up the beach as my eyes close of their own accord.

***

"Please, miss, just let me take you in for a check-up."

"I don't need a check-up," I argue, my voice finally back enough that I can be heard, "and my name is Libby. Libby Reed, I'm twenty-five years old. It's Wednesday the fifth. I'm fine. I swear."

"*Libby*." The older gentleman in the back of the ambulance levels me with his stare. "I don't think you realise how close you came to losing your life out there. You need to get checked out properly, by a *doctor*."

I shudder at the word. I hate hospitals. I hate doctors. "Can't you just treat me here?"

"I'm confident your ribs are broken. You need x-rays. Medication... things I can't give you."

My voice shakes as I shake my head. "I don't want to go."

He sighs heavily. "I'm going to go and see if I can get someone else to talk some sense into you."

I woke up as they were loading me into the back of the ambulance. I pitched a fit, and I've been begging them to take care of me right here in the five minutes that have followed.

A hospital is the last place I want to be.

They ask questions at hospitals; they want to know medical history, emergency contacts... all the things I don't want to talk about.

He disappears and within thirty seconds, he's back. The guy from the boat – *Rhett* – at his side.

My belly flips at the sight of him. He's shirtless, dripping wet and looking concerned.

He approaches me slowly. "Hey, sweetheart. Everything okay?"

I nod, my head screaming in protest.

"She won't listen to me, Rhett. I need to take her in."

He doesn't answer him, his attention firmly on me.

"Hi, I'm Rhett."

"Hi," I whisper.

"I understand that you don't want to go back to the hospital, but I really need you to, okay? We worked really hard to keep you alive and I'd like you to stay that way."

He runs his hand through his wet hair, his fingers pulling on the longer strands, and I don't know what it is about this guy, but my resolve wavers... the word 'yes' hesitates on my lips.

"I... I..." I stutter, and he steps closer to where I'm seated.

"Rhett!" a voice yells and he spins around in a flash, on high alert.

I freeze as a pretty brunette runs towards him, the camera I saw on the beach following behind her.

I hear Rhett sigh, but he walks away from me, towards *her*.

I try to tell myself that it's the camera that scares me, but I think there might be more to it – I think if I'm honest, the woman making heart eyes at him is bugging me just as much.

"I'm Emily Simons, reporting to you live from Howard Beach, I'm here with Rhett Jensen..."

Everything fades out as the camera does a slow sweep of the carpark, stopping on me, sitting in the back of the ambulance.

She said *live* TV.

Live. As in, on air *right now*.

Here I was thinking that the videos people are probably sharing on social media and YouTube were my biggest concern. I was wrong.

My blood runs cold.

"Turn it off!" I scream as I scramble to hide.

Rhett spins around to face me, shock evident on his face. "What?"

"The camera!" I yell. "Get it away, right now!" I cover my face with a blanket at the same moment I hear Rhett say, "We're done, get that camera out of here."

My heart whooshes in my ears as panic sets in.

Live television.

"What's wrong?" a soft voice questions, *his* voice.

"Is it gone?" I breathe.

"They're gone. You're okay."

I don't know why I trust him, but I do. I tug the blanket slowly from my head, my eyes darting around to double-check before finding him again.

His eyes bore into mine. "You want to tell me what that was all about?"

I shake my head.

"They were just covering the rescue..."

"They had no right to film me."

"Okay. I'll talk to them."

"It's too late," I say, my tears falling now. "It's too late for talking."

He frowns, not understanding. *Of course* he doesn't, he's just some cute guy at a beach. He probably doesn't have a care in the world.

"I didn't ask them to do that," I whisper.

"You didn't ask us to save you either, but we still did it."

I nod. "You're right. I *didn't* ask any of you to do that."

He opens his mouth to speak again but I cut him off.

"I think I'll go to hospital after all," I tell the paramedic who's been sitting up behind me, probably wondering if I've got some type of head injury to make me so crazy.

He looks relieved.

I don't look back at the man who saved my life as I'm moved to a bed and laid down. I can't even bring myself to glance at him as one of the doors are swung shut, the other following, but I hear him when he says, "You know, most people just say thank you."

"Thank you," I whisper, even though I know damn well he can't hear.

CHAPTER THREE

Rhett

"You're late," my best bud, Calum, grumbles as I arrive.

He slides a beer down the bar, and I catch it, taking a long, well-deserved pull as I take a seat next to him.

"Sorry, rough day."

"Your speedo too tight?" He smirks.

"Yeah, they just don't make them big enough," I bite back.

He chuckles, sipping his beer. "You lose someone today?" he asks, genuinely this time.

There have been plenty of days where I've lost people on that beach, and those are the days that make me seriously consider why I do this job in the first place.

I shake my head. "Not this time. It was close, but I think she'll be fine."

My mind drifts to the woman I pulled from the merciless sea today.

She should just be another rescue, but for whatever reason, she's *not*.

I can't help but imagine her lifeless body in my arms, all the spark drained out of her. I can't stop thinking about her wide, golden eyes, filled with fear as the cameras rolled.

I can't figure out what it was all about, and there's nothing I hate more than an unsolved mystery.

"What's up then?"

I shrug. "I dunno... just an off feeling in my gut that I can't put my finger on."

"Probably that curry Ginny made us last night." He shudders, and I can't help but laugh.

His girlfriend, Ginny, is seriously the best. She's sweet, funny and she doesn't put up with any of Cal's crap – but the woman cannot cook for shit.

I shake my head, amused. "Can't be that, I fed mine to Cricket when Gins wasn't looking."

He scowls at me. "That explains why I was cleaning up dog puke at five this morning."

I tip my beer to him. "Guess I owe you one of these."

"Make it two. It was a hell of a lot of vomit."

I chuckle.

"How'd you go with renting the house?" I question.

Calum and Ginny have been neighbours for two years; they got together about a year and a half ago, fell in love and recently moved in together. Rather than selling Cal's house after he moved into Ginny's, they decided to rent his place out.

"Good, I think we got a chick from the viewing this morning. She's new to town, works at the library, so she shouldn't be loud and shit... Gins likes her, so I think that's all the boxes ticked."

"She know her new neighbour's like to get it on at all hours of the night? And that they're loud as hell..."

"She might have to learn that lesson the hard way." He smirks.

I lived with Calum for two years, I moved out and got my own place not long after he started dating Ginny – the two of them can't keep their hands off one another and as happy as I am for them, when you've just had your heart broken by your ex, it's too much to be around.

"You bought Ginny that ring she keeps hinting about yet?" I chuckle.

"Nope." He shakes his head.

I shake my head at him. "You should lock her in before she realises that you're actually a big dummy."

He shoves my shoulder. "I should... so that's why I bought her an even bigger ring than the one she keeps harping on about."

I choke on my mouthful of beer. "No shit?"

He grins. "No fucking shit."

I was just giving him a hard time; I had no clue he was really ready to take that step yet.

"Holy shit, man, congrats." I hold my hand out and he slaps his palm against mine. I tug him in and clap him on the back. "That's massive."

I know exactly how massive it is. I was ready to take the same step with Kelsey before it all went up in smoke.

"Yeah, it's actually why I wanted to have a beer tonight... break the news to you."

"Well I'm stoked for you, Cal, you two are going to be happy together."

"You'll be my best man?"

"Better check she says yes first." I smirk.

"You really think that woman is going to say no to me?"

I chuckle. As a matter of fact, I don't. Guess I'll be suiting up sometime in the not-too-distant future.

We shoot the shit and then make plans to catch up later in the week again before Ginny calls and Cal rushes off with his mind in the gutter.

Suits me anyway. I need to hit the hay, I can't put my finger on what's bothering me so much about what went on this afternoon, but I can't stop thinking about the woman I held in my arms and brought back to life when it was looking awfully damn bleak.

I push away the thought of her dying.

She's fine. She's going to be fine.

***

"Georgie, you hear back from Oscar?"

She shakes her head and I frown.

Oscar is one of the paramedics – the one who took away the girl I saved yesterday. We've gotten pretty well acquainted with the crews running the emergency services around this town – we deal with at least one of them on a daily basis.

If someone isn't drowning, then someone is drunk on the sand, or some dickhead is stealing bags, or a kid is lost... the list goes on. We even had to get the fire brigade down last week because some kid got his head stuck in the railing down on the pier.

Never a dull moment, that's for damn sure.

"Did you need to talk to that woman about something, boss?" Georgie questions me.

I shake my head. "Nah, I just wanted to check that he got her to the hospital okay, she didn't really want to go."

She looks puzzled but doesn't question me further.

I don't blame her for being confused. We never check up on the people we rescue. We do our job and then we hand over to someone else to do their job.

But this time was different. When Oscar asked me to come and convince her to see a doctor, I couldn't believe that she was refusing treatment in the first place.

It pissed me off a little bit if I'm honest.

I risked my life to save hers, and I didn't do that so she could go home at risk of something else killing her.

That all changed the second I saw her sitting there, clearly scared and obviously alone, her drenched hair falling like a thick curtain around her shoulders.

She was beautiful.

I shouldn't have thought about her like that, she was vulnerable, and I was at work, but I damn well still thought it anyway.

She was *gorgeous*.

The phone rings and I reach for it before Georgie can. "This is Rhett."

"Rhett, it's Oscar, you tried to get in touch?"

I turn away from the prying eyes of the junior guards. "Yeah, I ah... I just wanted to check on the young woman from yesterday, did you get her admitted okay?"

"Miss Reed?" he questions.

"I didn't catch her name."

"She's all good, Rhett, heard she checked out this morning and went home."

"Good, that's ah... real good."

"Should I ask why you felt compelled to check on this one and not any of the others? Wouldn't be on account of how pretty she was now would it?"

I glance over my shoulder at my company, who are trying and failing to look busy as they eavesdrop. "No reason. Just wanted to hear that you got her in alright after she put up a fight."

"I turned on the charm and she was like putty in my hands the rest of the way." He chuckles and I can picture his big belly shaking.

"Thanks, Oscar."

"Any time," he says before he hangs up.

I should feel satisfied now, but oddly, I don't.

I drop the phone back into its cradle.

"I'm heading down the beach," I tell the rookies. "Blake will be back from break in five."

They both nod, and I'm grateful that Nick is down on the beach and not in the tower – the guy would have given me a hard time about following up on one of our saves.

I do my best to think about anything but her as I jog down the beach and scan the waterline, but her golden eyes refuse to be forgotten.

CHAPTER FOUR

Libby

"Seriously, thank you so much for this. This place is amazing," I gush gratefully to my landlord and new neighbour. "I never even thought about the fact that I have no furniture, so this is exactly what I needed."

Ginny screws up her face. "I'm pretty sure that god awful couch isn't what *anyone* needs."

I giggle. She's not wrong, it's pretty ugly, but it's a couch, so it's more than I had before.

"It's not that bad."

She gives me a look that says, 'are you serious?'.

"Alright, it's hideous, but I appreciate it all the same."

"We'll go shopping for a couch cover or some throws or something," she says as she fusses over the curtains.

"*We?*" I question, confused.

"Oh yeah, didn't I tell you? We're going to be *best friends*." She grins so wide, I can't help but join her. "And best friends don't let their friend have an ugly couch."

I laugh. "It's really not a big deal."

"It *so* is. That couch is the reason I made Calum move in with me, instead of the other way around – that *thing*," she nudges it with her toe, "doesn't fit in my living room – so problem solved."

I stifle a laugh. It feels weird to laugh, especially so genuinely and with someone I really could see becoming a friend.

"We're going shopping – don't even try and argue."

"Wouldn't dream of it," I reply.

God only knows I could use a friend. I haven't had a real friend in a long time, maybe not ever.

"How old are you anyway?" she asks me.

"Twenty-two."

"Well I'm closer to thirty than I am twenty, so you've got me beat there."

"Are you and Calum married?"

She shakes her head. "Not yet, but I've been dropping hints about rings for the past two months, so watch this space."

She makes me smile. For such a small woman, she's got such a big personality.

"What about you? Have you got a boyfriend?"

I shake my head quickly. "Nope. No boyfriend."

I don't like being asked personal questions, but that's one I can answer honestly.

"How long have you been in town for?" she asks, making herself comfortable on the couch she hates.

"Ummm, a couple of months, I guess? I've been working at the library for about six weeks now."

"Have you checked out the beach? It's to die for."

I swallow the lump in my throat.

I've checked it out alright, and she's got no idea how accurate her description is.

I didn't tell her what happened last week after I first viewed this place. We've talked on the phone several times since, but there was no way I was going to embarrass myself with something like that.

"Yeah, I like to swim, but I haven't been down for a while."

I'm not sure I'll ever be able to show my face at Howard Beach ever again, not after the way I performed – not that I wouldn't do it again to keep my face off the TV.

I spent hours watching the news and scouring online news sites, and I haven't managed to come across the live footage of me nearly drowning even once, so I'm finally starting to believe, after a week having passed, that maybe I got a lucky break.

"Tell me more about your job. Any hot book nerds hanging around?"

I twist my hair around my finger nervously. "I haven't really been looking."

"Girl, why not? You should be dating."

Dating is the absolute *last* thing I should be doing. It's way down at the bottom of the list – right after sticking pins in my eyes.

"I'm not really looking for a guy right now..."

"Well you should be! You're young, hot... you know what? I'm going to find you a man."

My eyes widen as I take in the mischievous expression on her face.

"Oh no, that's okay, I'm really not interested."

"Are you a lesbian?"

I choke on air. "N...no? What?"

"You know... into chicks. It's cool if you are, I just need to know if I'm looking for eggplant or taco, ya know?"

I gape at her. I think I might have to revisit this whole friendship thing.

She giggles. "Oh relax, don't look so scared."

Scared. Now there's an emotion I'm accustomed to feeling.

"No dating. *Please*," I beg. "And for the record, girls don't do it for me. But neither do guys right now either, okay?"

She pouts.

"If you let it go, I'll go shopping with you," I bargain.

"Oh fine." She rolls her eyes. "But you're coming for dinner on Friday night at my place so we can celebrate you moving in, and I won't take no for an answer."

"Fine." I hold up my hands in defeat, happy to have avoided being set up, for now at least. "I'll be there."

***

"Seriously, Libs, taste this. My man makes a killer stir-fry."

I don't know when she decided that she was going to start calling me 'Libs', but I kind of like it.

Makes me feel like we're really friends.

I sit down my glass of wine and take the spoon she's holding out to me.

"Mmm," I moan, "that's *really* good."

Calum smirks. "I know, and serious warning, don't ever eat anything that Ginny makes, because it's *actually* a killer – like you'll die from ingesting it."

I giggle as she elbows him in the ribs. "Oh shut up, it's not that bad."

He shoots me a 'I'm not kidding' look behind her back.

I already learnt this lesson the hard way unfortunately; she bought me over a loaf of banana bread yesterday, and when I bit into it... I'm pretty sure she'd used salt instead of sugar.

Even the birds wouldn't eat it.

"Don't listen to him, he's just got a weak stomach," Ginny grumbles.

There's a knock at the door and I glance over my shoulder warily.

"Stop making fun of me and go get the door." Ginny shoves Calum in that direction.

I give her a questioning look.

"Oh sorry, I forgot to tell you that a friend of Calum's was joining us."

"Oh... okay."

I hear the two guys talking in the living room.

I'm instantly nervous. I'm out of my comfort zone just being here, no matter how welcoming Ginny and Calum have been – but now I have to meet someone entirely new, and there's always that fear in the back of my mind that something, someone, *somehow*, might tie me to my past.

"Don't look so worried it's just–"

He comes into view, his arm slung casually around Calum's shoulders, and my insides flip.

I couldn't forget that face if I tried.

"Rhett," I whisper at the same time she says his name.

His eyes flicker to mine, like he can sense me staring at him or he heard my whispered word.

He looks as surprised to see me here as I feel seeing him.

Ginny's babbling on about something, completely oblivious to the tension in the air.

Rhett ignores her, and approaches me slowly, like I'm a baby animal that might bolt.

"Hey," he says softly.

"Hi."

"How are you?" he asks, his warm eyes grazing over every inch of me.

"I'm fine," I whisper.

"Why do I get the feeling you two know each other?" Calum asks, breaking the spell swirling between the two of us.

"I ah... I..." I stutter, my eyes darting between the three sets on me. I don't want to tell them about my near drowning. It'll cause attention, and if there's one thing I hate, it's being in the spotlight.

Rhett's eyes search mine, and I don't know what he sees but he comes to my rescue, yet again. "I was on guard the other day and she cut her foot on a shell – I sorted her out with a band aid."

"Yeah." I smile tightly. "Rhett was very helpful."

"A band aid. You're such a hero, bro." Calum chuckles at the same time as Ginny says, "awww that's so sweet."

"I didn't catch your name though," Rhett says, his deep voice pulling me back to him.

Holy cow. The eye contact. So. Much. Eye. Contact.

"*Libby*," I breathe.

"Libby," he replies, smiling, and I feel it in every single inch of my body.

He's even more attractive than he was at the beach, and that's no small feat.

His hair is curly now that it's dry, longer on top and short at the sides, and my fingers are just aching to feel if it's as soft as it looks.

I can see a hint of the tattoo that I know covers his shoulder; in fact, I think I can make out the faint outline through the white t-shirt stretched tight across his chest.

"I knew you were doing important work down there but fixing boo boos for pretty girls is really fulfilling work. I'm proud of you, watch."

Rhett chuckles ignoring his friend's teasing.

"*Watch*?" I find myself asking. "Why'd he call you that?"

"Like *Baywatch*," Calum answers before Rhett gets a chance.

A smile tugs at my lips. I'm getting the impression that Calum is one of those guys that thrives on giving his mates a hard time.

"Because he's an *asshole*," Rhett provides. "That's the answer to why Cal does most things, Libby, because he's an asshole."

Ginny flicks a tea towel, hitting Rhett on his ass. "Stop insulting my boyfriend and go set the table you two. Me and Libs need to have a little chat."

My mouth goes dry, and Calum chuckles and shoves Rhett out the door.

His eyes don't leave mine until he disappears from sight, and even then, I swear I can still feel them on my skin.

"You better start talking Miss 'I'm not looking for a guy', what the hell was that?" She points an 'I mean business' finger at me.

I busy myself tossing the salad that's already been tossed. "*What*?"

"Don't give me 'what'." She nudges me with her elbow. "You and Rhett? That was some serious chemistry."

I feel myself blush.

"It was nothing, he just helped me down at the beach the other day."

"Don't bullshit me."

I gape at her, the utensils falling from my hands.

"I'm not, I..."

She giggles. "You should see your face; you're like a deer in headlights. You like him, admit it."

I don't want to admit *anything*.

"I don't blame you, he's *so* gorgeous."

Gorgeous. Dangerous. They both look the same to me.

"He is," I agree, throwing her a bone.

It's becoming obvious to me that I won't be getting out of this kitchen unscathed, so I figure I may as well admit to finding him physically attractive – that's hardly giving her much of anything. Even if I *was* into girls, I think I'd still find Rhett ridiculously hot.

"He's a sweetheart too, a really good guy," she carries on.

"I'm sure he is."

She drops the wooden spoon she's been stirring with, splattering sauce everywhere, and turns her attention to me, her hands on her hips.

I wince at the mess, but Ginny doesn't even seem to notice.

"But?" she prompts.

I frown. "Huh?"

"I feel a 'but' coming on... so '*but*' what?"

"But... I'm seriously not looking for a guy," I admit sheepishly.

She rolls her eyes dramatically. "I'll tell you what, I'll let this go for two weeks. Two *whole* weeks and then I'm not taking no for an answer, okay?"

I don't know whether to start planning my move to a new town or get on my knees and thank the lord for giving me a two-week amnesty – something tells me Ginny doesn't cut people a break very often.

She extends her hand out to me, and I shake it despite knowing it's going to come back and bite me in the ass later. "Deal."

CHAPTER FIVE

I still can't believe it's her – *she's* the new tenant in my best friend's house.

The woman I've been dreaming about for a week straight with no god damn reprieve – the one I thought I'd never see again is right here in front of me, and now that she is, I don't know what to do about it.

She giggles softly at something Ginny says, her honey hair falling across her face, and she flicks it back behind her, assaulting me with her mouth-watering scent.

Strawberries and cream.

That scent has been haunting my dreams.

"Rhett?" Ginny's voice snaps me from my daydream, and I shake my head, still dazed.

"Sorry, *what*?"

Ginny smirks knowingly. "I was just saying that Libs has been working at the library, did you know that?"

She lifts her brow at me, like she's helping me out in some way with that piece of information.

"Ah... that's cool, do you like it down there?" I ask, hating the way my stomach flips when she finally looks at me.

Makes me feel like a pussy and an excited teenager all at once.

She lifts one of her slender shoulders. "I guess it's good."

"You guess?"

"I mean, it's good. I like books…" her sentence trails off, her cheeks blushing.

God, she's fucking adorable. Shy as hell. Sexy as sin.

"I like books too," I reply.

"Since when?" Cal chuckles.

My fist darts out, connects with his shoulder and his laughter dies off.

"Dude, what the fuck?" he demands.

"Just because you don't know how to read, doesn't mean I can't."

He snorts, laughing at me. "You're so full of shit."

He's right too – I'm totally full of shit. I haven't read a book since high school, but whatever, I don't give a fuck. I'd say anything if it meant she kept talking.

I'm about to go for round two of awkward conversation with Libby when she stands, running her hands down the jeans that are clinging to her like a second skin.

"I think I might call it a night."

Ginny pouts. "You can't leave me here with these two; I need you to help me level out the boy-girl ratio."

I stand too. "Actually, I'm going to head off too, Ellie will be waiting on me."

"Oh good." Ginny claps her hands, seemingly over her pity party. "Rhett, you can walk Libs home."

"Oh that's okay, it's not like it's far." Libby argues, but she's wasting her time arguing with Gins, the woman *always* gets her way.

"Nonsense, it's dark out there, you never know who could be lurking around."

"That's just great, Gins, make it sound like we live in the ghetto why don't you?" Calum shakes his head in disbelief at his girlfriend.

Ginny rolls her eyes as Libby edges towards the door. "Don't be stupid – this is the safest neighbourhood around, but they're both going the same way so..."

"It's fine, Gins," I say, leaning down to kiss her cheek, "I'll walk her home."

Libby looks a mix of bewildered and anxious, and I don't blame her – Ginny is a force to be reckoned with.

"Tell Ellie I say hi," Cal quips.

"Will do," I reply with a roll of my eyes.

We say our goodbyes and then it's just Libby and me on the front porch.

I wave my hand for her to go ahead but regret it as soon as my gaze lands on her curvy ass in those damn jeans.

I jog down to catch up with her, and she glances up at me, looking even more nervous than before.

"So... how are you really doing?" I question her as we stroll down towards the front gate side by side.

"Thanks for not dropping me in it back there... I just I..."

"Don't want them to make a big deal over it," I finish for her.

She nods.

"You still didn't answer my question."

She peeks up at me, her eyes wide before dropping them back to her feet. "I'm fine. They did a few checks at the hospital, but I'm okay. No broken ribs, no damage to my lungs... just a few bumps and bruises."

I feel a weight lift off my shoulders, a sense of relief washing over me – I didn't realise just how badly I needed to see her well with my own two eyes until this moment.

"They said it would have been a very different story if you guys hadn't got to me when you did."

I shudder thinking about the sight of her head bobbing, sinking under. A few more seconds and she could have been gone.

She stops walking, and it takes me a moment to realise we're already at her gate.

"I'll walk you to the door," I say.

Anything to get a bit more time.

She doesn't argue, walking through the gate when I hold it open for her.

The dim streetlights make it hard for her to find the right key, and I hold my hand out to take them from her. "Let me."

She looks wary but drops the small bunch of keys into my waiting palm.

I find the familiar key right away and slide it into the lock for her.

I swing the door open and reach inside, flicking on the porch light. "You should leave that on the sensor setting."

"How did you..."

"I lived here with Cal for a couple of years," I explain. "I know my way around this place like the back of my hand... so if you ever need anything..."

She gives me a small smile. "Right. Um... thanks."

I blow out a breath. This is the moment where I need to leave, but I really don't want to.

"It was really good to see you again. I'm glad you're doing better."

She steps towards her door at the same time I move, our chests colliding.

I reach out to steady her, my hands landing on her shoulders. "Sorry."

She pulls away abruptly, like I've burnt her, and I frown.

"Sorry, I didn't mean to..."

"It's fine." She smiles tightly as she steps around my frame, giving me a wider berth this time.

I don't know what the hell I did wrong, but she looks like she can't get away fast enough.

"I'll leave you to it."

She nods.

I step down off her porch, frowning to myself. There's something about this woman I can't put my finger on, but I'm determined to figure it out.

"Rhett?" she calls after me.

My pulse skyrockets at the sound of her saying my name.

"Yeah?" I ask, turning slowly back to face her.

"Thank you. For the other day. For saving my life. I didn't say thank you and I should have. I'm really glad you were there."

I'm glad I was there too, but if there's one thing I hate, it's praise, it makes me feel like a hero, and I'm nothing of the sort.

"Just doing my job," I reply.

***

"Man, have I got the opportunity of a lifetime for you..."

I shouldn't ask. I *really* shouldn't. When words like that come out of Calum's mouth, it's rarely a good thing, but honestly, I don't have the energy to fight him on it. We both know he'll get his way eventually.

I'm exhausted. I haven't slept well in what seems like forever – in reality it's only been a couple of weeks – but the last full night's sleep I can recall having was the night I had dinner with him and Ginny... with *her*.

I'm in a slump and I'm completely and utterly certain about the cause of the problem.

A certain golden-eyed woman with hair like honey is plaguing my mind.

No matter what I do, I can't shake her from my thoughts.

She's like one of those annoying kid's songs that just plays on loop through your mind for days.

"Hit me with it," I reply as I take a long pull of the cold beer I've been hanging out all day to drink.

"Ginny wants to set you up with one of her friends – some chick from work or something."

I raise a brow at him. "Come again?"

"You heard me."

"Oh I heard you. You hit your head on the way over here?"

"Oh c'mon, man, you've barely dated since that bitch walked out on you, just find your balls and get back in the game."

I flip him off – not because he's wrong about Kelsey, but because I don't need the reminder of my own stupidity.

"I've dated," I reply gruffly.

"You went out on one date, once. *Dating* is plural. As in two or more."

"Thanks for the English lesson." I drain the last of my beer and signal for the bartender to bring me another one.

"So it's going to be a double date–"

"It's not going to be anything if I don't say yes," I interrupt him.

"You and I both know you're not going to refuse the opportunity to sit across from me all night."

"Who am I meant to be dating? Some chick? Or you?"

He chuckles and winks at me. "Play your cards right and I might let you get to first base."

"You're a sick man." I smirk.

He looks way too pleased about that.

"Just ask me when and where because Ginny already has this whole thing set up and I'm too chicken shit to tell her that I couldn't get you to agree."

It's my turn to laugh now.

Fucking Ginny.

"I'll owe you, big time."

I groan. "When and where?"

He stands up from his seat, pleased with himself. "Peggy's at seven."

He slaps a twenty down on the bar and starts to stroll away.

"Hold up," I call after him, "Peggy's at seven, *when*?"

"Tonight." He smirks.

I spin on my stool. "Tonight? You're fucking with me, right?"

"Wish I was, princess, but you've only got two hours to get home and make yourself all pretty, so you better bounce."

I put down my still half-full beer and follow after him. "Did you just say 'bounce'?"

He chuckles.

"Dude, stop!" I grab his shoulder and halt him. "I don't even know who the chick is. Shouldn't I know that?"

"It's called a blind date for a reason, watch."

"This is fucking *unbelievable*."

I run a hand through my hair and blow out a deep breath.

A blind date is quite possibly the last thing I feel like doing, but if it takes my mind off Libby and the inexplicable pull I feel for her, then maybe it's a good idea to give it a shot after all – god knows I need to do *something*.

"A chick she works with?" I question warily.

"That's what she said."

"*Fine*," I grumble. "I'll see you in two hours."

He just grins, the smug fucker, and whistles as he walks away.

Fuck. My. Life.

CHAPTER SIX

Libby

I watch as Ginny bounds down to her gate, whips around the path and skips towards my front door.

"Shit," I mutter.

I'd bet my last dollar that I know what she's here for.

She's been marking off the days on the calendar, counting down until she gets to play cupid.

It's been two weeks, but I'm not any more ready to be set up than I was fourteen days ago.

I know Ginny a lot better now than I did then though, so I'm well aware that she won't take no for an answer. She never does when it's something she believes in. Surprisingly, I'm also more confident and comfortable around her than I ever thought possible.

She knocks on the front door, and I stay as still as I can.

I might be more confident, but I'm still not *that* confident.

If she thinks I'm not home, maybe she'll go away.

She knocks again, and I throw up a silent prayer for someone up there to help me the hell out.

"I know you're in there, Libs! I saw you watching me through the window!"

Of course she did. The woman is as sharp as a tack and as quick as a cat. I bet she eats the businessmen she works with for lunch.

"Just give up, Libby-Lou..." she calls, clearly enjoying herself as she uses the nickname Cal has lumped me with.

I groan and move for the door, swinging it open. If I don't let her in, she'll probably just let herself in anyway. It's not like she hasn't got a key.

She smirks, victory written all over her face as she brushes past me, pausing to smile at the couch that's now completely covered with throws and cushions.

I shut the door and resist the urge to smack my head against it.

"I need you to go and get ready, we're going out tonight."

No time for small talk apparently, looks like we're just diving right in.

"We're going out *where*?"

"Peggy's, this little Irish pub downtown."

"Who's going to be there?" I ask, narrowing my eyes.

She shrugs nonchalantly. "Just some people."

"Which people?"

"What's with the fifty questions?" she asks sweetly, like butter wouldn't freakin' melt.

"You know *exactly* why I'm asking."

She makes a humph noise and sits her hands on her hips. "*Fine*, you caught me. I invited a guy for you to talk to. But you can't even be mad, because we had a deal, and tick, tock, two weeks is up."

"I don't think I'm ready for it, Gins, seriously, it's been a long week... I'm really tired."

I'm actually no more tired than usual, given that I spend most of my nights wide awake, flinching at every little noise, but she doesn't need to know that.

"You'll be fine after a few drinks."

"*Ginny...*"

"*Libs...*" she mimics. "Pleeeease, I need you to come. Me and Cal haven't been out in forever, and I really need a night on the town."

She rushes over to me, clasping my hands in hers.

"You don't need *me* for that."

"But it will be so much more fun with you there."

I doubt that. Being fun isn't exactly a defining quality of my personality, but she's turned on the pleading puppy-dog eyes now, and much like everyone else, I can't say no to her for long.

"I bet I'm going to regret this." I sigh.

She bounces up and down in excitement. "Is that a yes?"

"No." I scowl, trying not to smile at her antics. "It's an 'I didn't have another choice.'"

"I'll take it." She beams. "And before you ask, this is a *blind* date – I'm not going to tell you who it's with, so don't waste my time asking... we have work to do."

I groan.

"Now, let's go upstairs and see what sexy little outfits you've got hidden away."

She drags me up the stairs and I'm thankful as hell that all she'll see is clothes and not the secrets that I have hiding in my closet.

***

This is a seriously bad idea. I don't even recognise myself right now – and not just physically, although after the way Ginny dressed me up like a Barbie and coated me in eyeliner, I barely know the person looking at me in the mirror. But it's more than that. The woman that arrived in this small town a few months ago would *never* have agreed – albeit reluctantly – to go on a blind date.

I don't know what to make of it, but I have to hope that it's a positive change and not the biggest mistake of my life.

My spine tingles as we walk through the crowded bar, out to the back where they have tables and chairs set up for eating.

I spot Calum and he waves to me, his grin wide and easy.

It makes me feel a bit better about the situation, that is, until the man sitting opposite him gets to his feet and turns to face me.

His brows furrow and then relax as he quite literally drinks me in, his razor-sharp stare starting at my toes and slowly making its way to the top of my head.

"Rhett? *Really*?" I hiss at Ginny.

The traitorous cow just laughs as she leaves me high and dry, skirting around Rhett to get to Calum.

Rhett steps towards me, and as pissed as I am at Ginny and Cal for stitching me up like this, I can still appreciate just how delicious the man before me looks in his black button-down and grey jeans.

"Hey," he whispers when I stop in front of him.

"Hi."

"You look... you..." he stammers. "There aren't words, Libby, you look *incredible*."

I feel my cheeks colouring, his compliment heating me up both inside and out.

"I'm really sorry about this, but I think we've been played." He grins good-naturedly and I want to be wary, I really do – but it's hard when he looks so perfect, so sweet and charming.

"I think you might be right."

He reaches for my arm, then thinks twice about it and drops his hand to his side.

I feel relieved and disappointed in the same second, but he moves on so quickly, I don't have time to dwell.

"It's my fault, they want to help me get over my ex."

"Your ex?" I ask, cocking my head to study him.

He nods. "Ended badly a while back and they've been trying to get me to date ever since. I know it's a big ask, but do you think you could play along, help get them off my case for a bit?"

When he puts it like that, it doesn't sound anywhere near as scary... and his expression is so hopeful, I'm not sure I have it in me to say no.

I fidget, shifting my weight from foot to foot. "I mean... I guess I could..."

He smiles so wide it takes my breath away.

"You're a lifesaver."

I huff out a little laugh. It's ironic, given that *he* is the lifesaver, not me.

He reaches for my elbow, slowly, tentatively, like he's somehow aware of my fears and giving me time to back out, but when his skin brushes mine, I wish I could feel it forever.

"Wait." I halt him as he leads me towards the seat. "What about Ellie?"

I haven't forgotten about the girl he had waiting for him at home the other night.

"Ellie?" he questions, his expression perplexed.

"Yeah, what does she think about you going on a date with me?"

He chuckles, the laugh deep, coming from right down in his belly.

"I like you, Lib."

I feel my cheeks heat all over again at his casual use of a nickname.

"And I think Ellie – *my cat* – will be just fine with it." He winks, and I want to curl up and hide for the rest of my life.

His cat. Ellie is his freakin' cat.

Could this get any more humiliating?

"Oh my god, I'm such a loser." I cover my face with my hands.

He waits patiently for me to get over my embarrassment, then grins, stealing all my air once again. "I'm a one-woman kinda guy, Lib, I promise. Cat excluded, of course."

"Of course," I mutter, my cheeks still burning hot.

He gestures for me to slide into the booth ahead of him.

I shoot Ginny a 'you're so dead' glare and she smirks back, tapping her watch for emphasis on the fact my time is up.

Stupid Ginny and her stupid deals.

Calum launches into a story about something that happened to him at work today, and before I know it, I'm sipping on a glass of wine and actually enjoying myself.

Ginny leans into Calum's shoulder in a fit of laughter, and he looks down at her with such tenderness it makes my heart hurt.

He catches her eye and they share a moment so sweet I have to look away.

I hadn't noticed Rhett move closer to me, so when he leans down and speaks into my ear, it startles me.

"I'm really glad you're here," he says.

Butterflies go crazy in my stomach as I brave a glance at those deep, brown eyes.

"I'm having fun," I reply quietly.

"So am I."

I don't know why he makes me feel so nervous, so out of control.

"I guess going on a date with me wasn't so bad after all."

My eyes widen. "What makes you say–"

He grins good-naturedly. "I saw that look on your face when you saw it was me you were here to meet."

I feel like a complete asshole. "It wasn't personal, I was just... *surprised.*"

"It's all good, Lib, I wasn't expecting you either... but it was a pleasant surprise."

I swallow slowly. I feel it coming before he even says the words. He's going to ask me out. He's looking at me like he wants to know me, the *real* me... and that's not an option on the menu when it comes to me.

I could do *this* when we're just humouring Gins and Cal, but not the real thing. I'm not ready for the real thing.

He opens his mouth and here it comes. "I was just thinking... maybe you and I coul–"

"I have to use the bathroom," I blurt out, interrupting him.

"Ah... okay?" He frowns. "Right now?"

I nod furiously, my heart pounding. "Right now."

He slides out of the booth, and I rush away as fast as I can, looking like a complete psycho, no doubt, but what else is new?

The poor guy is probably back there wondering where the hell he went wrong, meanwhile I'm over here looking like I'm about to crap my pants.

What a night.

CHAPTER SEVEN

Rhett

"Did she just *literally* run away from you?" Calum asks, bewildered.

I sit back down, completely confused by the sudden turn of events.

"I think so."

"Dude, what the fuck?" he demands.

I gape at him. "It wasn't *my* fault."

"No, it's *not* your fault," Ginny reassures me. "You've been nothing but sweet. She's just kinda flighty. I haven't been able to get anything about it out of her yet."

She frowns like it greatly displeases her.

I rake my fingers through my hair, my feet itching to go after her.

Christ, if Ginny hasn't got answers, then I haven't got a shot in hell. This girl must be locked down tighter than Fort Knox.

"*Exactly*," Calum drawls, "he's being *too* sweet. Haven't you heard the saying 'treat 'em mean, keep 'em keen'?"

"You're an *idiot*." Ginny rolls her eyes.

"Got you, didn't I?" He smirks.

"She makes me nervous, dude." I huff out a breath, running my hand through my hair again.

"So you *are* into her?" Ginny asks softly.

I meet her eyes. "I couldn't be *more* into her and she couldn't be *less* interested."

"Tough break, watch," Cal quips.

Ginny elbows him in the ribs. "Would you just shut up for five seconds?"

He shrugs, smirking. "Probably not."

She ignores him, turning her attention back to me. "Don't give up too easy. You're a good guy – she'll see that if she lets herself hang around you long enough."

I don't know what it is about this girl, but I'm borderline obsessed. Thoughts of her drive me insane every waking minute. Actually, that's a lie; it's not just every waking minute, because every night when I fall asleep, she's there in my dreams too.

I don't know what the hell I'm meant to do about it. She's making it clear she wants nothing to do with me, yet I see her when she doesn't know I'm watching. I see the way she turns her body towards mine on instinct, before she catches herself and moves away. I don't miss the hitch in her breathing when I say her name or the way she blushes when our eyes meet.

I think she's more interested than she's letting on, but that doesn't explain why she just bailed on me like I had an infectious disease.

Ginny shoves Calum and he stumbles out of his seat. "I'm going to go check on her," she announces.

I throw a balled-up napkin at him as he sits back down, watching Ginny walk away. "You're a jackass, you know that? You could have told me it was Libby I was meeting tonight."

He leans back, his arms splaying wide. "Didn't know, swear to god, Gins is a master at pulling the wool over my eyes."

"Fucking Ginny," I grumble.

"Why are you so weird about this girl?" he asks, suddenly taking an interest.

"I like her, but I dunno, man... she seems *vulnerable*. I just need to know she's okay."

He leans forward, resting his elbows on the table in between us. "What don't I know?"

"It's nothing." I shake my head.

It's no use now though; he's like a dog with a bone when it comes to getting information out of me.

I rake my hand down my face. "If I tell you, do you promise not to tell Gins?"

He ponders it for a minute. "I'll do my best, man, but she has these... *methods* of extracting information from me, if you know what I mean?"

I chuckle. "Forget it."

"No, no, no," he answers quickly, "I can be strong. I've got this. My girlfriend doesn't own me."

I don't know if the pep talk is for his benefit or mine.

"I mean it, Cal, this stays between us."

"Scout's honour."

I know for a fact that he was never a boy scout, but it's going to have to do.

"The other day when I met her at the beach–"

"When you played hero with a sticky plaster?" he cuts in, amused.

"Yeah... that's not exactly how it went down."

"Enlighten me then," he prompts.

"She was drowning... I had to swim out and pull her from the sea."

The smart-ass grin slides off his face. "Fucking hell."

I nod in agreement, shivers racing over my skin.

"She wasn't responding when we got her to shore, she'd swallowed some water, probably wound up with a few bruised ribs from the compressions, but she was lucky, man, really lucky."

"Lucky *you* were there," he breathes.

All the shit he gives me about *Baywatch* and speedos is all in good fun, and even though it drives me insane, I almost prefer it to the look he's giving me right now. It's the hero look.

"It was a team effort," I mumble.

"You saved her life."

"Whatever, man, it's not the point. I just *can't* forget her – I can't get her out of my head. All I see is those golden eyes and her sweet smile."

He leans back in his seat. "You're so screwed."

"I know I am, dip shit, that's what I'm telling you. I want to know more about her, but she keeps running."

"So, what are you going to do about it?"

"Well I was going to ask my best mate for advice, but apparently all he's good for is pointing out the obvious."

He grins. "I don't know what to tell you, Ginny just turned into a puddle of mush at my feet – I'm not equipped for dealing with women that aren't interested."

"You're so full of shit."

He chuckles. "Seriously though, maybe you just need to be patient... keep trying to talk to her?"

I blow out a breath. It's starting to feel like that might be my only choice.

***

The beach is quiet today, which is weird as hell for a Saturday, and I don't like it – it feels off and when things feel off, that's usually when shit starts to go wrong.

Even more wrong than your blind date going to the bathroom in the middle of the date and never coming back.

I do my best to push the disappointment away.

Ginny text me later that night to make sure I knew it was nothing I'd done wrong – Libby just needed some space apparently.

Space from *me*.

I didn't need to be a genius to read between those lines and see that was what she was really trying to say.

"What's up with you, boss?" Nick asks as we both scan the waterline.

"What makes you think anything is up with me?"

"The fact that I know you."

Nick and I have worked together the longest of all the team, he's my second in charge and he's right, he does know me – it's why I've been avoiding working in close proximity to him all morning.

"Girl trouble," I mutter.

He nods knowingly. "Tough break."

"You have no idea."

He doesn't push it further and I'm grateful, the last thing I want is him knowing the trouble I'm having is with the women I plucked from the sea only a few weeks ago.

I go back to checking the beach.

There's fuck all happening down here, and as grateful as I am that no one is in danger, it's going to be a long-ass day at this rate.

I'm considering going for a swim to test the conditions when I hear Nick mutter a string of curse words under his breath.

"Uh... Rhett..." he says, his tone sounding panicked.

"What is it?" I demand, grazing my eyes over the swimmers again, searching for the danger he's spotted.

"I think your girl troubles are about to get ten times worse."

I pull my focus from the water to glare at him, and that's when I see what he's talking about.

I just can't catch a damn break.

My gut was right after all. My day *was* destined to turn to shit.

Kelsey waves at me, her body clad in nothing but a barely-there bikini, and I curse the day she ever crossed my path and sunk her claws into my life.

She sucked me in hook, line, and sinker and then chewed me up and spat me back out.

"Bitch," Nick mumbles as she approaches, and I have to agree. It's a pretty fitting description of my ex-girlfriend.

"I'm gonna take a walk," he says, giving us some space, heading in the opposite direction.

I nod. No sense in both of us having to deal with her.

I go back to looking at the sea, unwilling to let my eyes linger on the curves I know so well.

"*Hey...*" she coos as she approaches, "long time no see, babe."

She rests her hand on my forearm where it's pressed firmly across my chest.

My head snaps towards her, staring first at the bright green eyes I used to be so in love with, then to the perfectly manicured nails that are touching my skin.

I was once so into every single part of this woman, wanted to spend the rest of my life with her, and now I feel nothing but disappointment when I look at her.

If I had it my way, I'd never have to lay eyes on her again.

I step to the side and her hand falls between us.

"What do you want, Kelsey?" I drawl, bored.

"I just came to say hi, you don't have to be such a dick," she snaps at me, losing her fake-nice façade for a fraction of a second before slipping her mask back in place. "I miss you, babe. I miss *us*."

I know exactly where this is coming from. Word on the beach is that her new boyfriend dumped her last week. This has got nothing to do with me, or *us*, and everything to do with *her*. As per fucking usual.

She's selling bullshit again, only this time I'm not buying it.

"You miss *us*?" I ask gruffly.

She sidles up to me again, her boobs brushing my arm. "I do, babe, don't you miss me too?"

I choke out a humourless laugh. "That would be a no."

"You don't even miss me a little bit?" she purrs, undeterred.

She walks her fingers up my arm in an attempt at seduction, but all it achieves is making my stomach roll. I can't even look at her.

Good to know.

I might not be enjoying going to bed alone every night, but it's nice to know my body is setting the standard well above *her*.

"Hard pass."

She makes a stroppy, frustrated growl. "You're such a dickhead, Rhett Jensen, it's no wonder I walked out on you."

"I'm at work, Kelsey, can you take your drama somewhere else?" I huff out a breath, tired of her crap – even though I can't deny her words sting deep down.

"I can't believe I ever wasted my time on a loser like you."

"Tell someone who cares."

She shoves past me and storms down the beach as I watch out of the corner of my eye.

The bitch might be a pain in the ass, but it was worth that little encounter just to see her get so mad.

She storms past Nick, further down the beach. He flips her off, and she kicks sand in his direction, nearly tripping over in the process.

I crack a grin as he howls with laughter.

Definitely worth it.

CHAPTER EIGHT

My heart pounds as I scream again, the pounding on the front door still not relenting.

"Help!" I scream at the top of my lungs.

Ginny and Calum live so close, surely they can hear me, but I've been screaming for five minutes and nobody has come to save me yet.

I spot my cell phone on the bed and leap towards it like a lifeline.

I hit call on Ginny's name.

"Hey, girl, what's up?" she asks casually, like my life isn't flashing before my eyes.

"I need help, are you home?" my words come out in a rush, barely making sense.

"Libs?" she questions, the line crackling.

"Oh my god, where are you?" I squeal hysterically.

"What's wrong?" she demands.

"Send Calum over, I need help!"

"We're not home, what's... are... okay?" The phone cuts in and out.

"Ginny?!"

"Mother-in-law... out... town... visiting..."

I fall over in my panic, and I scream again.

I hear Ginny say my name but when I look down at the screen, the line has gone dead.

I try to take a deep breath, but it's no use – I'm freaking out.

I tap Ginny's name again, but it's engaged.

"Oh my god, oh my god, oh my god," I whisper to myself.

This is it. This is the moment it all ends.

My eyes dart to the window, and I consider jumping out of it, but I'm on the second floor and I'm likely to break my ankles, and then it'll just make finishing me off even easier for him.

Think. I tell myself.

I need a weapon. I have to find some way to defend myself when he gets in here.

I rush from where I'm standing on the bed and into the closet.

The best I can find is a stiletto heel with a sharpish point, so that's going to have to do.

I try Ginny once more, but it won't connect at all now, and when I try Calum, I get the same. They don't even have service. I'm all alone.

I could call the police, but they'll never get here in time anyway.

I sprint back across the room, stiletto still in hand and dive onto the bed, pulling the covers up high over my head.

If I just lie here and be quiet, maybe it'll all be over soon.

I hear my breath, ragged and rough in the small tent I've made myself.

There's nothing but silence in the house that seems to stretch forever, and it scares me more than the idea of loud noises. At least you can hear those coming.

There's a noise that sounds like a creaky stair and tears start streaming down my face.

I knew this time would come, but even with the amount of time I've had to prepare for it, I'm still not ready. I don't want it to be over. I finally like my life.

I'm considering the window again when I hear my name, and not *just* my name, but my name being screamed at the top of someone's lungs.

From *inside* the house.

I hear feet landing heavy on the stairs – the sound unmistakable, and then my name again, "*Lib*, where are you, sweetheart?"

Oh my god. It's Rhett. I shouldn't recognise a virtual stranger's voice like that, but I do.

He's here.

"Libby?! Fuck, where are you, baby?"

More heavy feet.

More yelling.

Doors opening and closing.

My breathing turns into heavy pants under the covers. He just called me sweetheart *and* baby.

I hear his footsteps coming down the hallway, coming closer.

"Watch out!" I yell.

He's going to wind up hurt, or worse. All because of me.

This is even worse than being here alone. I don't know what I was thinking calling Ginny before, the last thing I want is for anyone else to be in harm's way.

"*Lib*," he says, his tone relieved when he hears my voice. He tries to open the door, but it hits the heavy chest of drawers

I managed to push in front of it in an adrenaline-fuelled moment.

I sit up in the bed, the covers falling away from my face, tears still running down my cheeks.

I shouldn't feel safe now that he's here, but the truth is, that's exactly how I feel.

"Get out of here, Rhett, there's–"

He shoves the door again and the dresser rattles. "Are you okay?" he demands.

I don't answer.

"Libby! I need to know what happened."

"There was a man," I whisper.

"*What*?" he asks, still trying to get in.

"A man," I half shout. "He came up the path, pounded on the door. I locked it, but I think he's in the house, you have to get out of here."

The shoving stops. And he's quiet for a beat. "You locked the door behind you?"

"I locked it and ran straight up here."

"It was locked, baby, it was still locked," he says, his tone relieved.

"But you got in," I insist, still panicked, "If it was locked, how did you get in here?"

"Spare key under the red pot." He pushes the door open the fraction that he's been able to budge it. "Let me in, Lib."

"No! He could still be out there."

"There's only me, I promise."

"You don't know that; you'd have to search the whole house."

"Alright," he replies, the shoving stopping.

"You mean it?" I ask softly.

"Of course, baby, just hold tight, okay? I'm going to go and look around."

"Okay," I squeak, a fresh wave of tears threatening.

"I'll be right back," he promises.

I nod.

"Rhett?" I ask quietly even though I'm not sure he's still there.

"Yeah?"

"What are you doing here?"

"Ginny called me. Her connection was bad but I heard enough. She said you were screaming. I thought someone was hurting you. I think I probably broke about one hundred road rules on my way over here."

I bite down on my lip. Unsafe driving aside, that's the sweetest thing anyone has done for me in a long time.

"Rhett?" I ask again.

"Yeah, Lib?"

"Thank you."

***

He hands me the steaming cup of coffee and sits down on the now not-so-ugly couch with his own cup.

"Thank you." I smile softly at him.

"You're welcome," he replies, and I can tell he's still thinking about the disaster of an afternoon.

I go to take a sip, but stop myself. "I'm really sorry, *again*."

"It's not a problem, honestly. I'm just glad you're okay."

Wow. There he goes with the eye contact again.

I dip my head in embarrassment, not just because I'm shit scared of a postal delivery man, but because when he looks at me like that, it's too easy to imagine what kissing him might be like.

The thought doesn't terrify me nearly as much as it should.

"You sure you're alright?"

I'm not sure I'm alright at all. I haven't had a panic attack like that in years, but when I saw that man running towards me, I freaked out.

"I think I'll be okay."

He sips his coffee, all the while eyeing me carefully.

"Where'd you come from, Libby Reed?" he asks.

It's a question that sets off alarm bells – deep seated panic in my gut, but I can't let him see that, I have to play it cool.

"I'm from all over really, I've been on the move as long as I can remember," I reply vaguely.

"So she's a traveller." He grins, his eyes sparkling.

I smile when he does. I can't help it. He's really sweet, too sweet – it's making it hard to keep a safe distance from him.

"You planning on sticking around here long?"

As long as I feel safe.

Or until someone comes looking.

"As long as they'll let me." I shrug, the truthful answer coming off as light and playful even though it's anything but.

"What about you?" I ask. "How's a guy like *you* wind up single with a cat?"

Shit. I just complimented and insulted him all in one breath.

He chuckles. "It's just one of those things I guess; wasted too much of my time with the wrong girl, and by the time I figured that out, it was too late."

I know a little something about giving the wrong people too much of your time.

"And the cat?"

"Ellie just turned up one day. She was a stray and I dunno... I guess she never left."

I can relate to that too.

I'm pretty much a stray too.

"It was good of you to take her in... looks like you make a habit of coming to the rescue."

"I've got a radar for a damsel in distress." He grins boyishly, and my heart skips a beat.

It only took Rhett about five minutes to determine that the man jogging up my pathway towards me was a delivery man – the card to collect a package that was taped to my front door was a dead give-away – but it took him at least another thirty minutes to coax me from my room, along with a struggle to get the dresser moved far enough that he could squeeze through and put it back against the wall where it belongs.

He's a whole lot of man to squeeze in.

Turns out no one was after me. No one was in my house. There was nothing to fear. Rhett didn't once give me a hard time about it, instead he just offered his hand for me to hold until I calmed down.

Ginny called about twenty minutes ago in a complete panic, and I was too embarrassed to tell her what really happened, so it was Rhett to the rescue again, spinning some story that didn't make me sound like the complete and utter head case that I am.

He really is making a habit out of saving me. He even offered to set up a camera system out front so I could see who was at my front door before answering it.

In one afternoon, he's done more for me than anyone in my old life ever did.

Twenty-two years' worth of effort all exceeded in the space of a few hours.

"You think you'll be alright here on your own now? I better head back down to the beach and check on the guys."

My cheeks flame red. "You left work to come here?" I squeak as he stands.

"It's no big deal."

It *is* a big deal. It's a *very* big deal.

I can't believe he did that. For *me*.

He stretches his legs, gets to his feet, and I follow him towards my front door, still at a loss for words.

"If you need *anything*, just call me, we're right around the corner – me and my cat." He smirks. "I can help with anything you need, Ellie too, she's always up for sorting out rodent problems," he says, his tone light but his expression serious.

He can't even imagine the kind of help someone like me might need, but it's sweet of him to offer nonetheless.

He pauses, waiting for me to acknowledge what he's said.

"I don't know how I can possibly thank you."

I can feel his stare right down to my toes. "You could let me take you out on that date."

My breath gets caught in my throat.

I want to say yes, a huge part of me is screaming the word, but the rest of me has a hand firmly holding the handbrake.

"*Rhett*, I..."

He steps closer to me, his hand slowly coming up to brush my cheek, the back of his fingers just ever so gently grazing my skin. "You don't have to say it," he whispers, "you're not ready, for *whatever* reason, and that's okay. I'm not going anywhere. I'm a patient man."

I can't breathe.

I can't think.

I can't even move.

"Goodbye, Lib," he says, and just like that, my knight in shining armour strolls out like he didn't just steal a little piece of my heart.

CHAPTER NINE

Rhett

Shelf after shelf of books stare back at me, taunting me for not knowing what the hell I'm doing here.

I only just figured out the difference between fiction and non-fiction, yet I'm scanning the shelves like I have something specific in mind that I'm looking for.

I guess I do have something specific, only it's not something I'm going to find in a book.

My guess is that I'd find her at the checkout desk, or stocking the shelves somewhere, but I figure if I don't want to look like a desperate stalker, then I at least better take a book up with me.

I slide one from a shelf and do a double take at the cover. It's a dude chewing on some chick's neck, but weirdly, she looks like she's enjoying herself.

I put that one back and keep walking down the aisle.

The word thriller catches my eye.

I can do a thriller.

It's a romantic thriller, but still, it'll do. Half an hour of wandering around this library is enough for me given that I'm here for the girl, not the books.

I take my time finding the checkout counter, scanning every row of shelves for a glimpse of her honey-coloured hair.

I round the corner, and there she is. My heart rate takes on a new rhythm, beating in a sequence that only occurs when she's near.

I don't know what it is about this girl, but I'm *drowning,* and I don't want to be saved.

She's checking out some books for a sweet-looking little girl with blonde pigtails, so I hang back, watching her from a short distance. She's so into her chat with the little girl that she hasn't noticed me yet.

They're talking about dinosaurs.

"My favourite is the T. rex," the little girl says.

"The T. rex is a great choice," Libby replies.

"What's yours?"

She thinks for a minute. "You know, I've always loved the Ankylosaurus."

"That is a good one."

"Ella! I've been looking all over for you." A blonde woman rushes over. She looks just like the little girl, minus the pigtails. "*More* dinosaur books?"

"I was right here, Mumma."

"Sorry, Sara, she told me you said it was okay." Libby winces.

"Oh, it's not your fault, Libby, you know how this one is with her books."

The two women exchange an amused look and the child stomps her foot.

"They're new, Mumma, I *needed* them."

Libby's watching her with an expression that tells me she loves kids, even mid-tantrum.

"You've got enough. They have a limit for a reason, honey."

Libby slides the stack of books across the counter and stage whispers, "I won't tell if you don't."

I know I've got a stupid grin on my face; I can't even explain what's put it there other than *her*. She affects me like nothing else I've ever come across.

We both watch the mother and daughter leave, a stack of dinosaur books with them, and then finally, her eyes lift, and she sees me.

She gasps and it does crazy shit to my insides.

I push off the shelving I was leaning on and close the distance between us.

"You know, I was really hoping to brush up on my prehistoric knowledge, you'll have to tell me when your little friend returns those books."

"What are you doing here?" she breathes.

I hold up the book and then sit it on the desk in front of her. "Just grabbing some light reading."

Her gaze bounces between the book and me.

"Told you I like books."

Her brows rise and the corners of her mouth threaten with a smile. "Uh huh."

"Have you read this one?" I ask her.

She bites back a smile. "I have."

"What's that look for?"

She shakes her head. "Nothing... just, you'll see I guess... if that's the one you're going with?"

I pick the book up and look the cover over again, eying it sceptically. "I think I can handle it."

She looks amused – cheeky, and hell I like it on her; playful suits her.

My smile is wide as I hand her the book, our hands brushing, sending sparks up my arm.

She's all of a sudden incredibly busy on her computer.

"Library card?" She holds out her hand, and I frown.

When I don't pass her anything her eyes meet mine.

I grimace sheepishly.

"You don't even have a library card, do you?"

"Busted."

She tries to bite her lip to contain her grin, but she can't. She smiles at me, and I swear to god, the sun pales in comparison.

"So maybe I don't read all that much," I admit.

"I'm sure we can change that."

When I leave, ten minutes later, it's with a smile on my face, a spring in my step and a shiny new library card tucked into my wallet.

***

"Where have you been? Ginny has been hassling me for the past half an hour," Calum whines as I let myself into their house.

I drop the three books I checked out prior to coming here onto the hall table.

I've been to the library every few days for the past two weeks.

I've never read so many books in my life.

"You think you were coming to book club or something?" He flicks through the books in amusement, holding up a romance book that I let Libby talk me into. "*Saucy*." He smirks.

I snatch it out of his hands and put it back at the bottom of the pile.

"I just came from the library, couldn't be bothered walking home first."

"The library again, huh?" He waggles his brows at me as I follow him into the kitchen where Ginny's mixing something in a bowl.

Calum goes and takes over – thank god, because I'm starving.

"Hey, Gins." I lean in and kiss her cheek, and she wraps her arms around me for a hug.

"Stop macking on my girl," Cal grumbles.

"It's not my fault she can't keep her hands off me."

He flips me off, Ginny smacks my shoulder lightly, and I chuckle.

"How was Libs today?" she asks me.

I frown, confused about how she knows where I've been.

"I heard you two girls talking about books, so you must have been to see Libby, *again*," she explains, gesturing between Cal and me.

"I went for the books," I argue.

She rolls her eyes. "*And…*"

"And Libby was good, really good, actually." I smile to myself as I think about how much she's relaxed around me since I started dropping into the library to see her, because who am I kidding? It was *never* about the books.

"You've got it *so* bad." She grins victoriously as Cal laughs and mutters something about me being whipped.

He's one to talk. The guy is *owned* by Gins.

She claps her hands gleefully, and I shake my head in amusement. If this thing between Libby and me ever goes anywhere, I can guarantee that Ginny is going to take *all* the credit.

"Have you asked her out again yet?"

I shake my head. "Nope."

She smacks my shoulder again. "Why the heck not?"

"Because I'm trying this thing where I *don't* come on too strong... you should try it sometime. Who said I was going to ask her out anyway? Maybe I just want to be friends?"

"*I* don't need any tips, thank you very much, she already likes *me*. And friends...? Oh *please*."

"No fighting, ladies," Cal chimes in.

Ginny grins at me and I just want to tackle her to the ground and give her a noogy. She's always felt like the little sister I never had. The incredibly annoying little sister.

She pokes out her tongue at me, just to hit my point home.

"Seriously, you should ask her out again, she seems like she's finally settling in here."

"I'll ask her out when I'm good and ready and not a minute before."

She grins like the cat that got the cream. "But you *will* ask her out again."

"Do you practise being this irritating, or does it just come naturally to you?"

"It's all-natural talent." She smirks.

"You've got a gift," I mutter.

She skips over to the fridge, pulls out two beers, opens them and hands one to each of us.

I slump into a chair as I take it from her. "Thanks, Gins."

"See? You love me really."

That girl is going to give me whiplash one of these days.

"Nick was telling me about how Kelsey was down the beach the other week," Calum says. "How'd that treat ya?"

"Nick needs to learn when to shut his mouth," I grumble. "And it treated me about as well as a knee to the balls."

"*That* bitch?" Ginny squawks. "What the hell was she doing there?"

"It's a public beach," I remind her.

"I don't give a shit if it's public. She knows damn well that's *your* beach."

I huff out a laugh. *My* beach.

"It wasn't a big deal. She came along, strutting her stuff and thinking I was going to come running back now that she's single again."

"*And*?" Ginny prompts.

"And she was fucking wrong."

Ginny smiles wide.

"I'm never going anywhere near that toxic bitch ever again."

"Praise the lord," Calum chimes in.

I flip him off.

"You're going to be so much happier with Libby, I can feel it." Ginny sighs.

"How many chickens, Gins?"

She frowns at me in confusion. "Huh?"

"I figured you must know how many chickens there were, given that you're counting them well before they've hatched."

"Oh, ha ha," she says with a dramatic roll of her eyes. "Mark my words, Rhett Jensen, you two have got big things on the horizon."

I huff out a laugh and take a long pull of my beer.

I hate to admit it, but for once, I hope Ginny is right.

CHAPTER TEN

Libby

"Next," Ginny prompts, and I try to relax my fingers so she can paint the next nail bright pink like the others.

"Sorry," I mumble as my finger flinches, "I'm not very good at being pampered."

She smiles as she looks down at the tiny brush coating my nail with polish. "It's fine, I'm just going to have to whip you into shape."

I don't doubt that for even one second.

I've already been dragged along to countless shopping trips, coffee dates and now she's ventured into giving me the full manicure and pedicure experience, right here in the middle of her living room while Cal watches the game.

I'm actually starting to love our girls' trips, but telling her that would only encourage her further, so I keep my trap shut.

"How's work been lately?" she asks absently.

I want to spill my guts, tell her that it's been the best few weeks I've had in a really long time, that having that sweet, sexy man drop in to see me puts the biggest smile on my face and that the highlight of my day is watching his perplexed expression when I recommend a new book for him to read.

I want to giggle about the way his tongue peeks out from between his teeth when he focuses on the words on the back of a book, or how his shirt rides up when he stretches to get a book from the top shelf.

But I *can't*.

That's how normal girls talk about guys, and there's nothing much normal about me.

I'm not one of those women who can give herself to a man, especially not one like Rhett – I'd only end up breaking both of us.

No matter how much I might want to get closer, the best thing Rhett could do is stay far, far away.

"It's been good," I say instead of all the things I'd rather say.

She taps my next nail and gets halfway through painting that before she moves onto what I know is the real reason she asked about work.

"I heard you've had a repeat visitor?"

I nibble on my bottom lip. "He keeps showing up."

"That's because he likes you."

My stomach flutters at the idea. I'm not an idiot. I know Rhett is interested. I'm damaged, not stupid.

"He barely knows me," I argue.

"Well maybe you should give him a chance to then."

"A chance at *what* exactly?"

She glances up at me and winks. "I bet he'd be up for just about anything when it comes to you. You two would be so hot in bed. I'd put money on it."

"Ginny!" I hiss, my eyes darting to see if Calum is listening.

"Oh don't even worry about it." She goes back to painting my nails, the second coat this time. "He doesn't listen to a word I say when the game's on."

"Are you sure?"

"Positive. Right, babe?" she asks loudly, "you wouldn't mind if Libby and I got nude and wrestled in the middle of the room?"

Calum doesn't even budge. His eyes stay glued to the television like Ginny never even spoke at all.

I giggle. "Alright then."

"So back to Rhett... why are you still turning him down?"

"I'm not technically *still* turning him down... he hasn't asked again lately."

She snorts. "That's a bullshit technicality and you know it."

I scowl at her, but it doesn't last long. Her no-nonsense attitude always has me smiling.

"What's really going on with you, Libs?"

She sits down the little bottle of polish and turns her full attention on me.

My heart races as she assesses me carefully.

"Nothing." I swallow nervously.

"Right, and I was born yesterday."

I consider telling her everything, but I can't make the words come out. It's too risky.

"I don't want to talk about it."

"*Libby*?" she questions, laying her hand on top of mine and squeezing. "You know you can tell me anything, right?"

"He scares me," I whisper.

"Oh, Libs, he'd never lay a finger on you, he's not that kind of guy."

"I know," I admit. "And *that's* what scares me. I'm starting to trust him, and I haven't trusted a man since I was eighteen years old."

She frowns and I can see she's about to bombard me with questions, but I've already said enough – too much, in fact.

"I don't want to talk about it," I repeat.

She nods, still frowning, but surprisingly, she doesn't push for more.

"*Fine*. I won't ask, but I think you should give him a chance, he's a really good man, Libs, one of the best, and I think you two would be really great together. Everyone needs someone... maybe you need him."

He *is* a good man, a great one, even. He's shown me already that he'll keep showing up for me, that he's not going anywhere, and as much as that scares the shit out of me, it also makes me doubt the way I've distanced myself for the past few years.

Maybe she's right – maybe I do need someone.

Rhett is attentive, sweet, kind and of course, completely and utterly gorgeous.

"I'll think about it," I whisper.

I've been thinking about it for two weeks straight – I can barely think about anything else, but from now on, maybe I'll consider it in a different light... one where I share all of me.

She grins, somehow sensing that my walls are down the lowest they've ever been.

"FUCK'S SAKE, GET THE BALL DOWN!" Cal screams, flying off the couch and scaring the crap out of me and Ginny.

My heart pounds as hysterical laughter bubbles out of me.

He rants and raves, curses and mutters, until he's sitting back down again, his gaze never once even flicking to us.

Ginny shakes her head in disbelief. "Next time he's watching a game, I'm coming to *your* place."

***

I sense him; know he's there before I even turn around.

It's like I can feel his eyes burning up every inch of my body – that, and I've been not-so-patiently waiting for him to turn up for his regular Friday, four-thirty visit.

He comes straight from work on a Friday and it's my favourite day of the week – he smells like the beach, the scent of saltwater clinging to his golden-brown skin.

"Hey, Lib," he says, his voice deep and sexy as I turn around to face him.

I can't help it, my eyes give him a slow top to toe appraisal. I'm practically drooling when I'm done.

"Hey," I reply, my cheeks colouring when he grins at me like I've made his day just by existing.

"What have you got for me today?"

"Depends how you went with the one I gave you last time?"

I start walking and he falls into step next to me.

He doesn't answer and I risk a peek up at him. He's at a loss for words.

"Are you blushing?" I giggle softly.

"Hell yes, I'm blushing, woman."

I might have to give him more romance if that's the reaction I'm going to get.

"Did you read it?"

"I read it."

"And?"

"And it... it was *hot*."

I know just how hot it is, I've read it at least ten times myself. Escaping into a book is one of my favourite past times.

I'm not about to tell him, but I'm seriously impressed with him. I know he's not one of those guys who likes to read, but maybe I might have managed to convert him.

I hold my hand out and he passes me the book. "What now then?" I ask as I start to walk towards another set of shelves. "What about–"

His fingers catch on mine and gently pull me back to him. "What about you let me take you out?"

Those deep, complex brown eyes bore into mine, willing me to say yes.

He's still got hold of my hand as he steps closer, his other hand coming around my waist in a way that feels surprisingly welcome.

"Rhett," I whisper, leaning into him. "I'm no good for you."

"Why don't you let me be the judge of that?"

We're tucked in between two shelving units, hidden from prying eyes and it feels like we're the only two people here.

"Let me take you out, Lib... *please*?"

"Okay," I breathe, finally giving in to what I know we both want.

His answering smile is blinding.

His thumb softly moves up and down, rubbing my side and making me tingle.

"When?"

"I get off in..." I lift my hand to check my watch, his coming with it, "ten minutes... does that work for you?"

"That works for me," he replies quickly.

He holds me captive with those gorgeous eyes, and just when I think he's about to try and kiss me, he lifts our hands higher and presses the sweetest of kisses to my knuckles.

My knees go weak and my spine races with tingles.

I'm in so much trouble here. He's already closer than I've let anyone get since... since a time I don't want to think about. They all are; him, Ginny... even Calum are too close.

I like these people so much that the idea of having to move on and leave them makes me want to break down and cry.

I think I'd even miss Cal's big dumb dog.

"Has it been ten minutes yet?" Rhett asks, his excitement catching.

I giggle. "Not quite. I've got just enough time to find you another book."

He chuckles. We find him another novel, and after I'm done with my shift, he's still waiting right where I left him, leaning against the wall just inside the library door, reading the book he just checked out.

And my god, he's so life shatteringly sexy with his nose between the pages.

"All done."

He looks up to find me in front of him and his lips curve into a smile.

He always looks at me like I've just lit up the room. Like he's just seeing me for the very first time.

He slides his book into his bag and holds his hand out to me to take.

It's just holding hands. I coach myself. *Little kids hold hands.*

I press my palm into his and his long fingers weave through mine before he pulls me along behind him. "Let's go, we're going to be late."

"Late for what? I only just said yes."

He grins at me over his shoulder. "I've been waiting a long time for you to say yes, Lib, so if you thought I wouldn't have a backup date waiting, you'd be seriously wrong. Hopefully it doesn't disappoint."

I have a pretty strong feeling that nothing about the man in front of me could ever come close to disappointment.

But I can't help but think he might be disappointed if he knew the real story of me.

CHAPTER ELEVEN

Rhett

It's finally happening.

She said yes to me.

Her small warm hand in mine makes my heart race as we stroll towards my truck.

"I can give you a lift back to your car later. Is that alright?"

The grip on my hand tightens and then relaxes. "I ah… I actually don't have a car."

"You don't have a car? Like at all?"

She shakes her head. "I don't even know how to drive."

"Why not?"

She shrugs. "No one ever taught me."

"How do you get to work?"

"Walk or ride my bike," she replies, her tone shy, like she's worried I might think it's stupid.

I don't know what it is about her, but these little bits of information feel like parts of a much bigger puzzle. One I'm desperate to put together so I can see the finished product.

"I bet your carbon footprint is fantastic."

She giggles and the mood lightens.

I open the door for her, and she climbs in, biting gently on that delicious bottom lip of hers.

I drive us over to the arcade, park up and turn to her in my seat.

"It's a bit lame, but I always loved playing the arcade games... are you up for it?"

She shrugs, glancing around curiously. "I've never been."

I don't know where the hell this girl came from, but the fact that she's never played a bunch of overpriced kids' games with budget prizes is a situation that needs remedying, right now.

"Well then I'm about to rock your world."

She grins, catches herself and tries to bite it down, but it doesn't work, I see it. I see her.

I need to have a word with her parents; it seems like they neglected to give her some of the most simple experiences as a kid.

Her hand is back in mine and she's following me inside before I can ask any prying questions that I'm sure she doesn't want me asking.

If there's one thing I've learnt about Libby these past few weeks, it's that she's really good at talking, yet not saying much of anything.

She gives nothing away, and I can see she's fiercely private.

I'm cool with that, I *am*, what I'm not cool with is the look of unease and the fear in her eyes that only shows up when she thinks no one is looking.

I'm also not okay with the knot in the pit of my stomach that tells me the two things are directly related.

"Oh my gosh," she breathes as we walk into the huge room full of gaming machines, flashing lights and loud noises. "This is insane."

"It's crazy, right? I probably should have checked you didn't have epilepsy or something before bringing you in here."

She giggles softly. "You're safe there."

I nudge her leg with our joined hands. "What do you want to try first?"

Her eyes widen. "How are you meant to choose?"

I wink at her. "No idea. Lucky for you, we've got time to play them all."

She grins, so wide that a dimple I've never seen before appears in her left cheek.

I swallow deeply. Just when I thought she couldn't get any more beautiful.

I get her a card loaded up with credit and lead her towards the ball games. "Let's shoot some hoops."

I half expect her to say no, or to tell me to have the first turn, so when she pushes up her sleeves and grabs a ball, I'm seriously impressed.

I'm beyond impressed when her first shot sails through the small net.

"Look out LeBron James."

"I'm pretty sure they call that beginner's luck."

I grab another ball and hand it to her. "Let's find out then."

She wasn't entirely wrong. She makes only another handful of shots, but she's smiling so wide I can tell she couldn't care less.

She glances around the room, looking for what game she wants to play next – I know that feeling, these games might be meant for kids, but they're a rush.

"Want to try win one of those giant teddys?"

"Aren't you going to try and win one for me?" she teases, her expression coy.

Fuck yes I am.

I grab her hand, and she comes along with me, a spring in her step.

"Which one do you want, Lib?"

She giggles. "You're awfully confident for someone who doesn't have a key to the machine."

I smirk at her. "I've got a card loaded with credit and nowhere to be for the next hour and a half. Tell me which one you want."

"I'll take the pink one."

"Excellent choice."

It takes me close to forty-five minutes, but when we leave the arcade, it's with matching smiles and a ridiculously huge pink teddy bear.

And *yes*, like the guy behind the counter pointed out, I probably could have bought her a toy for less than what I spent trying to win the stupid thing, but where's the fun in that?

***

"We can go somewhere nicer if you want?"

She shakes her head, those golden eyes shining. "Pizza is perfect."

Pizza is in no way *perfect*, but after seeing how much she relaxed at the arcade, I decided to ditch my idea of a fancy restaurant and keep things casual.

I'd do just about anything to make her comfortable right now.

We get seated in a table over the far side of the restaurant. It's no private booth up the back, but it'll do.

"What kind of pizza do you like?" I ask as we scan the menus.

"Pineapple, ham and cheese."

"*Pineapple*? On a pizza?" I balk.

"Don't knock it until you've tried it."

"But it'd be *warm*." I shudder.

She giggles at my disgusted expression. "What kind of pizza do you like then?"

"Pretty much anything."

"Except pineapple." She grins.

"Except pineapple."

"What can I get you both?" The waitress appears, note pad in hand.

"I'll take the supreme, and this one wants the pineapple."

The waitress grimaces and I chuckle. "That's what I said."

"There's always one," she replies, teasing. "And to drink?"

We order a couple of cokes and then we're left alone again.

Libby glances down nervously as I openly stare, taking in every last detail of her face. I can't seem to control myself when she's around.

"Why'd you finally say yes?" I ask.

Her eyes snap up, surprised. "What?"

"To me... the date... what made you finally say yes?"

She lifts one shoulder. "Honestly, I'm not sure... I mean Ginny has been a pretty big cheerleader..."

"I'll have to buy her a set of pom poms."

She bites her lip, a grin pulling at the corners. "I guess I realised how much I liked seeing you since you've been coming into the library all the time."

I guess my persistence paid off after all.

"I haven't seen you back down at the beach."

She shakes her head gently and her cheeks stain with the blush that I'm coming to love.

"Why not?"

"Would you be caught dead there after making such a fool of yourself?"

I flinch involuntarily at the use of the word 'dead'.

"No one thinks you're a fool."

Her eyes soften, the gold burning brighter. "*You* more than anyone should think I'm a fool. But anyway, it doesn't matter, once bitten, twice shy and all that."

I'll get back to exactly what I think of her later, but one thing is for damn certain, she's no fool.

"You don't swim anymore?"

"I started going to the pool." She grimaces.

I smirk. "And how's that working out for you?"

"I hate it," she admits, her tone sheepish. "It's so hot and stinks like chlorine... I don't even want to think about what's in that water."

"You should come back to the beach, the saltwater is so refreshing and clean." I try to tempt her. ".. there's this good-looking guy patrolling the waves."

"I... I'm not sure," she says, her earlier playfulness gone.

She wants serious? I can do serious.

"Come with me one day. I'll keep you safe, Lib, I'd never let anything happen to you. I promise."

She searches my face, and I feel her probing at my statement, looking for any trace of a lie.

There's nothing to find.

I'd keep her safe no matter the cost.

I risked my life for hers when I'd never even seen her face – that's nothing compared to what I'd risk for her now.

"Why are you so good to me?"

I balk at her statement. I've done nothing that any decent guy wouldn't have done.

I've done nothing more than show up to see her and now take her out for a few hours. There's nothing impressive about that.

"You know I like you, Libby."

She blushes again, but this time doesn't shy away from my gaze.

"*Why?*"

Why what? "Why do I like you?" I ask, my brow furrowed in confusion.

She nods.

I don't understand the question. I'm completely and utterly baffled.

Does she not understand the appeal she holds?

Has she not seen a mirror lately?

Does she not see how sweet she is?

"You don't see yourself very clearly, do you?" I ask instead.

She frowns, her brows drawing together.

"You're beautiful, Libby, and not just on the outside... you're good to the core and you can't hide that from me. I see you."

Shit, I don't know when things got so heavy, but if a sappy speech is enough to convince her of how incredible I think she is, then fuck it, I'll happily hand over the man card Cal is always harping on about and shower her with romantic gestures.

Her mouth has fallen open and she's opening and shutting it like a fish, lost for words.

I can't help but chuckle, it's comical.

"Here we go," the waitress interrupts, sitting our food down on the table, effectively ending the conversation.

It doesn't bother me. We can talk about how great she is any time she wants; it's not like it's a challenging topic.

"Thank you," Libby breathes, and I don't know if it's directed at me or the waitress, but I'll take it. When it comes to this woman, I'll take whatever I can get.

"Tell me about your family," I say, thinking I'm switching to a light topic.

The look on her face assures me I was mistaken.

There's a fleeting look of sheer panic in her eyes that has the hairs on my neck standing on end, and then as quick as it came, it's gone.

"We're not close," she says, her voice controlled, measured.

"What's your favourite book?" I ask, doing a complete one eighty and hoping like hell she'll roll with it.

She smiles this time, and reaches for a slice of her pizza, the cheese hot and stringy, hanging from the slice as she brings it to her mouth.

I follow her lead and take a bite of mine, moaning in appreciation as the flavours hit my tongue.

"This is the best pizza," I say between bites.

She nods in agreement, sets down her slice and takes a sip of her coke. "My favourite book?"

I nod.

"That's like asking a mother which of her children is her favourite."

I chuckle. "I bet every parent has a favourite child, they just know they can't say it out loud."

She shakes her head, her eyes sparkling like she thinks I'm terrible.

"You must have a favourite," I press.

"I have lots of favourites, depends what mood I'm in."

"Right now?"

She smiles softly. "Right now... *Reckless Heart* by AJ Cole."

I catalogue it in my mind for future reference.

"Why?"

"You can take it home next week, then you'll see why."

My grin stretches wide, my mind eager for an insight into that mind she keeps so well guarded.

"Don't look so excited, it'll rip your heart right out of your chest," she warns me.

I don't even care. If it's happening at her recommendation, then I can live with that.

"Will it put it back in again?" I question.

"Maybe." She smirks. "But you'll just have to wait and see."

CHAPTER TWELVE

Libby

"And then what happened?" Ginny demands, her knees bouncing with excitement.

"And then he drove me home, walked me to my door, gave me a lecture about still not having the security light on and said goodnight."

"That's it? He didn't even kiss you?"

I bite my lip.

"He *did* kiss you?" She squeals, her keen eyes missing nothing.

"Only on the cheek," I mumble, embarrassed. "It was just a little peck."

"But?" she prompts, eyes wide.

"But it was still easily the best kiss I've ever had." I sigh, falling back against the couch.

This is so *not* me, this swooning, sighing girl, but right now, it feels like me. I like this. I like talking to a friend, a *real* friend about a guy I'm into. I've never understood those chick flick movies where the girls sit around talking about boys and braiding their hair, but here I am, and all I'm missing is the hairstyle.

I even bet Ginny would do it for me if I asked her to.

I giggle at the thought.

"Oh you *so* like him!" she says, grinning like a fool, "when are you going out again?"

I lift a shoulder. "I don't know, Gins... I'm not really in the best place."

She waves away my concerns with her hand. "Oh bullshit, you're in the perfect place. You've got a job, a good house, an ugly couch, the best friend a girl could ask for..."

Laughter bubbles out of me. "You're crazy, you know that?"

"I am and I do." She smirks.

My phone chimes with an incoming message and I reach over and grab it from the coffee table, a slow smile spreading over my face when I see whose name is on the screen.

"Oh, girl, you've got it bad."

I *have* got it bad – that's the problem. I'm smitten, but I'm also terrified.

I *can't* be smitten.

Smitten doesn't work for me.

Smitten means trouble.

"Don't do that," she says softly, all trace of humour gone.

"Do *what*?" I whisper.

"Get all lost in your head like that. I can see you overthinking it from a mile away."

I open my mouth to argue, but it dies on my lips. She's right.

I'm always overthinking, but in my world, where I come from, overthinking is what kept me alive. It's the only thing that put me far enough ahead of *them*.

"You know you can talk to me, right, Libs? I know I've got a big mouth and that I can be a bit full on, but I'm actually really good with secrets."

"I know," I whisper.

Her blue eyes search mine and she nods. "If you change your mind, you know where to find me."

She busies herself with a magazine, flicking pages aimlessly. "Are you going to check that text or not? The suspense is killing me."

My gaze flies back to the screen of my phone, excitement chasing my nerves away.

To: Libby
From: Rhett
How would you feel about being surprised?

I nibble on my lip. Normally the idea of being surprised would settle in the pit of my stomach like a lead brick, but when the idea is delivered from Rhett, it doesn't seem nearly as scary.

To: Rhett
From: Libby
I think I could be convinced.

To: Libby
From: Rhett
Good, give Ginny the green light and I'll see you soon, Lib.

My jaw falls lax as my eyes travel from my phone to my friend.

She waggles her brows at me. "Let's go, baby!"

She jumps up off the couch and heads for the stairs.

I rush after her once the initial realisation that I've been played wears off.

"How do you manage to have such a successful career and still find time to scheme with Rhett?"

"Oh, sweetie," she turns to glance at me over her shoulder as she steamrolls her way into my bedroom, "I'm a modern woman, I can do it all."

I can't help but laugh. There's nothing else for it.

I'm not going to be able to stop Ginny, that's for damn sure. All I can do now is hold on tight for the ride.

"What am I wearing?" I say with a roll of my eyes.

She's rifling through my closet now, tossing items she deems worthy onto the foot of my bed.

Bikini.

Denim shorts.

Tank top.

I take a deep breath in through my nose and blow it out my mouth.

I know *exactly* where we're going.

***

"You owe me." Ginny points a finger at Rhett as we exit her car.

I was right, here we are... at the beach.

The same beach where I nearly drowned.

Rhett grins and pushes off the block wall he's been leaning against, and I have to stop myself from drooling.

He's shirtless, wearing only a pair of shorts slung low on his hips and there is *so* much to look at.

He's all tight, toned muscle and sun-kissed skin.

He's got just the right amount of ink and that curly hair I've grown so fond of is still dry and falling in his eyes.

He chuckles at her and tries to ruffle her hair, but she ducks under his arm and skips off to where I can see Calum stretched out on a beach towel a short distance away on the sand.

He's surrounded by endless amounts of stuff; towels, a picnic basket, some type of game, body boards, and a huge beach shelter is off to his side with a table and chairs set up underneath it.

Out beyond the sand are the crashing waves, breaking on the shore. The sea that nearly took my life.

"I'm glad you came." The rumble of his voice comes at my side, and my eyes find his like they know the way by heart.

"I didn't have much of a choice," I admit.

He smirks. "Why do you think I left Ginny in charge?"

I poke him gently in his firm, broad chest. "That's a dirty trick."

He captures my hand in his and slips my palm into his, his fingers threading through as though he's done it every day for a hundred years.

"C'mon," he says, tugging my arm.

"I'm scared," I admit.

He comes back for me, standing right in front of me so we're toe to toe, his chin dipped to keep my eyes glued to his.

"I won't let anything happen to you. You don't even have to swim." His free hand cups my jaw and my skin pebbles under his touch. "Just spend the day with me, Lib, *please?*"

As if I could refuse him. I spent weeks giving it my best shot and look how that turned out – with me as putty in his hands.

I nod, too weak in the knees to speak, and he smiles like I've just told him he won the lottery.

He leans in quickly and kisses me on the cheek again, and I'm so caught off guard that when he tugs me along next to him I stumble a bit, causing me to blush and him to grin knowingly.

"Is that a volleyball net?" I ask, quirking a brow as my toes dig into the warm golden sand.

"Sure is."

"Don't even think about playing with them, Libs, they both played for the rep team in school and they're crazy competitive," Ginny drawls as she lathers herself in sun cream. "They'll tell you they want to play doubles and then they'll only hit it at each other." She pouts.

"That was *one* time," Cal whines, "and I had a point to prove."

Ginny starts arguing with him about it. Rhett just laughs and points out a spot for me to sit down.

He offers us all drinks and when his back is turned to get them, Ginny makes a show of gesturing to my clothes. More to the point, that I should take them off.

I scowl at her and almost get caught by Rhett as he passes me a coke.

"Thanks," I breathe.

He nods and drops down to sit next to me, and I'm suddenly very aware of just how little he's wearing. I can feel his body heat radiating from him, warming me all over.

Ginny tosses the sun cream at me. "Get your kit off, biarch."

Rhett busies himself with looking through a bag and I shoot her daggers.

"It's a beach," she says, her tone sassy, "no clothes allowed."

I roll my eyes but lift my top over my head anyway. That's it though. The shorts are staying for now – taking your clothes off next to a guy that looks like that is a risky little game.

I turn to grab the tube of cream and Ginny whistles.

"Girl, you've got a tramp stamp! Who the heck would have guessed?"

I feel Rhett's fingers every so softly skim over the skin at the base of my back and I shiver.

"How did I not see this until now?"

I feel myself blush as I spin back so it's not in their view. "It's nothing... a stupid teenage decision. We all do dumb stuff when we're sixteen."

Ginny starts babbling to Cal about some tattoo she's been wanting to get, and I hope like hell this is the end of that conversation.

I can feel Rhett's eyes on me, and I don't know what it is about him, but I welcome his stare.

I watch as one of the lifeguards on duty moves a flag along the beach then gestures for the swimmers in the water to move so they're back in the safe area.

"You didn't have to work today?"

"My first Saturday off all month."

"And you spend it down the beach." I giggle.

"I'm an addict."

Ginny and Cal are arguing about the volleyball game again, although it sounds more like flirty foreplay than it does a real argument.

"You surf?" I ask, tipping my head towards the few surfers out past the breakers further down the beach.

"A bit when I was a teenager, but I spent pretty much all of my free time competing as a lifeguard, so the surfing took a back seat."

"Competing?"

"Yeah, you know, surf swimming, beach sprinting, paddling board and surf skis... all the clubs in the country get together for events to compete."

"That's a thing?"

"Hell yeah it's a thing," he replies at the same time that Calum chimes in, "It's only a thing in his budgie-smuggling-wearing world."

"Do I even want to know what that means?" I laugh.

"Budgie smugglers are speedos," Ginny explains, "and ignore Cal, he's just jealous he doesn't have all those medals like Rhett does."

"And that he doesn't fill out a speedo as well," Rhett quips.

Calum stalks towards Ginny and throws her over his shoulder as she shrieks.

He slaps her ass as he jostles her around. "Whose side are you on, woman?"

Rhett chuckles next to me, the deep sound vibrating through my whole body.

"Medals, huh?"

He lifts a shoulder, his expression modest. "Might have a few."

I watch with amusement as Cal stalks all the way to the water's edge and deposits a still-shrieking Ginny into the shallow whitewash.

"What's your event?"

"I was a swimmer, but I was pretty fast across the sand too."

"You don't compete anymore?"

He shakes his head. "Nah I'm old and washed up now, Lib, I'll leave that to the young bucks."

He doesn't look at all old or washed up, not from where I'm sitting.

"You still swim though, right?"

He pulls his eyes from the sea and glances at me curiously. "Yeah," he finally replies, "I still swim."

His gaze drifts, but there's something about his expression that confuses me.

Maybe it was a dumb question. I mean he's a lifeguard, *of course* he still swims, but it seems like it was something else.

"What?" I ask.

He shakes his head. "It's nothing."

"You're not a very convincing liar."

He chuckles. "No, I'm not."

He's silent for a few beats. It seems like he's weighing up whether to say what's on his mind or not.

"*Well*?" I press.

"I swam out to you... *that* day."

He doesn't have to explain, I know exactly what he's refer ring to. A shiver races down my spine at the thought of it.

He swam out to me?

"But the boat..."

"I'd got your head above water and got you clipped up by the time the boat arrived, we got you in and Nick drove us back to shore. You weren't responding to me then, that's why you don't remember..."

A cold sweat breaks out on my skin.

"You swam all the way out there, for *me*?"

The waves were crazy that day – it's like the current shifted and the swell grew between the moment I left the beach and the time it took me to get past the breakers.

He shrugs his shoulders, as though saving lives is such an everyday occurrence for him that he doesn't think it's a big deal. "I called on Becca when things started to go bad – she's our human speed boat, but there wasn't time to wait for her."

"So, *you* went into that roaring sea and saved me?" I ask in awe.

It never once occurred to me that he'd been in the water for anything more than the time it took to swim to and from the boat.

I never considered what he put on the line that day.

His *life*. For *mine*.

"I was just doing my job."

I rest my hand on his arm and his eyes find mine.

He's so humble it's unbelievable.

"You risked your life to save me, Rhett, that's a *really* big deal."

He mutters something under his breath, and I can tell he doesn't know what to do with my praise. He's clearly uncomfortable with it, but I don't care. I need him to know how grateful I am for what he did – how grateful I am for *him*.

I lean towards him, unsure about what I'm doing until my tongue darts out to moisten my lips and I realise... I'm about to kiss him.

I feel a deep breath rush from him as our lips inch closer together.

Apparently, he's realised what's about to happen too.

My hand snakes up his arm and is tangled in his hair before the thought of doing it has even formed in my mind.

I've been imagining it for so long; the action has taken on a life of its own.

His hands find my waist, and I might have been the one to start this, but it's becoming clear he's going to finish it.

He lifts me clear off my towel and settles me in his lap, our lips still not meeting, foreheads pressed together.

I go willingly, eager for whatever part of him I can get.

I've never been this forward in my entire life, and yet, it doesn't feel forward enough.

I gasp as he somehow pulls me closer.

"You're something else, Libby, so beautiful, so brave," he murmurs, his fingers skimming my bare arms as he pins me to his broad chest, my skin heating where it meets his.

I want to tell him that I'm not brave, not even a little bit, but then his mouth is on mine and I feel brave, I feel invincible.

I tug his hair, and he moans, shattering the world around me.

My other hand finds his chest, exploring the bare skin, the hard planes as his lips own me completely.

He tastes like sunshine.

If I wasn't already sitting, he'd have just brought me to my knees.

I break away, desperate for air, but when I get it, it's nothing compared to the desperation inside me to feel his lips again.

He must feel the same way, because his mouth claims mine once more, gently this time, his kiss soft and sweet. He's the one to pull back, and I can't help but smile along with him when a grin tugs at his lips.

"I don't know where you came from, but I'm so glad you're here," he whispers, and for the first time in what feels like forever, I'm happy to be right where I am.

CHAPTER THIRTEEN

Rhett

"Well this looks awfully cosy." Cal's voice bursts the bubble that's formed around Libby and me.

The last two minutes have been nothing short of pure bliss, so of course, right on cue, my best mate is here to bring me back down to earth.

"Awwww, I *knew* you two would be perfect together," Ginny chimes in as she follows him up the beach.

I ignore both of them; the woman in my lap will have every single ounce of my attention for every moment that she wants it.

Libby tugs her lower lip into her mouth and her cheeks pink when she realises we've been caught. But she doesn't make a move to climb off me like I expected she would.

Calum wolf whistles and it takes all my self-control not to get up and kick his ass. I'm finally making some real progress with her – she's lowering her walls, and here this clown is, trying his hardest to get her to build them back up again.

"They're not even there, Lib," I whisper.

"Oh, but they are." She giggles softly and it's like a straight shot to my dick, which, rather inconveniently, is still positioned directly underneath her perky butt.

"Babe, can I have your hoodie, I'm freezing," Ginny begs Cal and I sigh.

I don't know what possessed me to make this a group date. I should have known they'd just kill the mood.

Libby giggles and lifts her leg to climb off me, but I grab her thighs and hold her close for one more moment.

She gasps, and I worry I've pushed her too far, scared her, but when those golden eyes lock on mine, I see *want*, not fear as she drinks me in.

I crash my mouth to hers again, not giving a shit about our friends, my work mates or anybody else for that matter. It's just her and me, and a moment I've been dreaming about for weeks.

"Dude, seriously, I'm happy for you and all, but there are kids here."

Libby pulls back, her chest heaving.

Perfect.

She's fucking perfection.

She slides off my lap, and I let her this time, turning my attention to my so-called mate as I snag her hand – desperate not to lose contact – and hold it against my thigh.

"You couldn't have stayed in the water for another ten minutes, could you?"

"Sorry that my presence is killing your buzz." Cal smirks.

Bastard doesn't look the least bit sorry as he flicks his dripping hair out of his face.

Ginny shrugs on his hoodie, looking downright thrilled with her matchmaking skills, and I'm too happy to care.

She can take the credit; I don't give a shit as long *I* get the girl.

"You're full of surprises, Libby-Lou," Cal carries on, making Lib blush. "I didn't think you had it in you."

I'm about to tell him to shut the hell up when his focus shifts to Ginny, who's just bent down to pick up whatever fell out of the pocket of his hoodie that she's put on.

He dives to the ground, grabbing the small box before she can.

"What the hell?" she demands as he nearly knocks her to the ground. "What's wrong with you?"

"Nothing," he mutters, tucking the box behind his back and turning to face her.

"Oh shit," I breathe as I see what he's got, "here we go."

I know exactly what that box contains. I don't know why the hell he's got it here at the beach with him today. The guy really can be a dipshit.

"Don't *nothing* me, Calum, I know you're hiding something from me."

"Just leave it, Gins, trust me," he replies, trying not to grin.

"What the hell is going on?" Libby hisses to me as Ginny plants her hands on her hips, a pissed-off look on her face as she stares down Cal.

I can't answer, I'm too busy trying not to laugh. I told him it was a stupid idea to take that thing with him everywhere he went.

Libby nudges my side and I lean down to whisper in her ear. "It's an engagement ring."

Her jaw falls lax.

I probably shouldn't be spilling the beans but screw it. I know Ginny, and she won't give up until she sees what's in that box. The cat won't be in the bag for much longer.

"*Trust you*? While you're standing there hiding things from me?"

"I'm not hiding things from you, babe, you don't want me to show you this right now. *I promise*."

Ginny's still glaring at him, her temper flaring. "*Really*? Because it sure as hell feels like I want you to show me."

Cal shakes his head, a chuckle falling from his lips as Libby and I watch on with rapt attention.

Apparently laughing was a poor choice on Cal's behalf because Ginny looks about ready to skin him alive.

"Hand it over, right now," she demands.

"You really want to see it?"

"Yes, *Calum*, I 'really want to see it'." She does a piss poor impression of his voice, and it doesn't help me contain my laughter in the slightest.

I earn myself a death glare from Gins and hold up my free hand in defence.

Not my circus, not my monkeys.

I'm not going to end up in Ginny's bad books because Calum is a moron.

"In front of all these people?" he taunts her.

She narrows her eyes at him. "Are you carrying around a sex toy or something?"

Libby stifles a giggle.

"Could be."

"*Whatever*. I don't give a shit. Just show me already," she demands.

"Whatever you say, babe."

He lobs her the box, and as her eyes follow it, he drops to one knee. She catches the box, opening it at the same moment she glances back at him.

"Oh. My. God," she breathes when it hits her.

Her hand flies up to cover her mouth and tears pool in her eyes.

Calum holds his hands up in an 'I told you' gesture.

"Say something," I hiss at him.

He flips me off, his eyes never leaving his woman, and in true Calum fashion, he keeps it simple.

"This isn't exactly how I planned this, but I love you, Gins. From the moment I saw you, I fell hard. You're my whole life, and I can't imagine my life without you. Marry me, babe?"

Ginny nods furiously, tears streaming down her face. "Yes!"

"Can I get off the ground? People are starting to stare."

She splutters a laugh as he rises, wrapping his arms around her.

This should hurt, seeing two people get the future I thought I had coming right around the corner, but these are my best friends and I don't feel anything but happiness for them.

Libby sighs next to me and leans her head on my shoulder as we sit back and watch Ginny and Calum's lives change forever.

I can't help but think that my life might be changing too.

****

My feet pound against the pavement as my music blasts in my ears.

I hate running, but it clears my head and keeps me in shape, so I do it anyway.

Some people crave this burn in their lungs, but not me, I crave normal shit, like a Big Mac.

I slow down to a walk as I approach Libby's house. I've been running past every day for the past month, always hoping to catch her out front in the garden or something, but I've never struck it lucky. Now I just wind up here on instinct, still hoping for an extra two minutes of her time.

Doesn't look like today is going to happen for me either but given that I've got her phone number now, and she kissed me yesterday, I'd say I'm past attempting to co-ordinate random meetings anyway.

I can't stop the grin on my face when I think about yesterday.

What a fucking day.

I got my first kiss with Libby – got to hold her hand all day too, Gins and Cal got engaged, and I felt like I was on cloud nine the entire time.

Lib wouldn't swim with me though, which I guess is fair enough.

She'll trust me enough one day to get back out there with me, I'll make sure of it.

I'm about to roll back into a jog when a dude catches my eye. He's just sitting in his car, hardly doing anything suspicious, but the fact that he's got his phone out, pointed in my direction, doesn't sit well with me.

I jog towards him and he waves out.

I pull off my headphones as he gestures me over.

"Sorry to interrupt your run, but this house, it's not up for rent anymore?"

I glance over my shoulder. He's pointing at Libby's house.

I shake my head. "Nah, man, sorry, got snapped up pretty quick I hear."

He nods, tossing his phone on the seat. "Oh well, was worth a shot. Good neighbourhood, this one."

"Sure is."

He nods at me and starts his car before driving off, throwing me a wave out the window.

I shake my head at myself as I head off down the street.

I've got to stop being so paranoid.

I think it's since Libby entered my life. I still haven't figured out why she lost it with the TV crew at the beach that day, or why she ran out on our blind date.

She was a different woman with me yesterday; more open, less timid. Even if she did refuse a photo for Ginny's Instagram.

Can't say I blame her; I wouldn't want my face splashed all over there for Ginny's thousands of followers to see. The girl spends *way* too much time on the gram. But with Libby, it's more than that. She seems like she's always looking over her shoulder, but for what? I have *no* clue.

It's making me jumpy though, I know that much.

When she looks over her shoulder, I look over mine, because whether she's realised it or not, if something is coming for her, then they'll have to get through me first.

I don't want to be one of those guys who lays claim to a woman, but I'm willing to make an exception for *this* woman.

She needs someone. She needs *me,* and I'll be damned if I'm going to let her believe otherwise.

CHAPTER FOURTEEN

Libby

To: Libby
From: Rhett
You owe me.

To: Rhett
From: Libby
For what?

I worry my bottom lip as I wait for his response, wracking my brain to think of something that I could owe him for.

Other than saving my life, buying me dinner, winning me a giant teddy and kissing me like he was starving...

The phone vibrates and I grab it in a flash.

To: Libby
From: Rhett
That book you made me read.

To: Rhett
From: Libby
Sorry! I did warn you.

A grin spreads across my face as I stare at my phone, waiting for him to reply. I can't believe he actually read that book.

To: Libby
From: Rhett
You don't look very sorry.

My head snaps up and my phone clatters to the desk in front of me.

Friday, four-thirty. On the dot.

"Hey, beautiful."

"H-h-h hey," I stammer, caught off guard by the magnetising force that is Rhett Jensen.

He sets the offending book down in front of me and leans slowly across the desk. He brushes his lips against my cheek, the small scrape of stubble against my skin making my insides quiver.

His scent surrounds me, drowning me, making me forget all reason and turning my brain to mush.

I hear myself sigh, one of those dreamy, *I'm in so much trouble* sighs.

He leans back, out of my space and I exhale in relief. Maybe I might have a shot at not sounding like a scatter-brained little girl if he doesn't stand so close.

Even now though, with a foot between us, he's still so distracting. All I've thought about since we kissed is *him*.

I lay awake at night – nothing new there – but instead of worrying, my head is filled with Rhett. The taste of his tongue, the softness of his lips...

I'm *addicted*, and that doesn't bode well for me.

He raps his knuckles twice on the cover of the book. "They should put a warning in the front of this thing. Damn near broke my heart."

"You'd have to be some kind of monster if it didn't," I tease.

He smirks and god he's gorgeous. "So I pass the test then?"

"I think you might have."

He definitely did. I know monsters, and Rhett isn't one of them.

"Good... so, about you owing me..." He grins wide.

I'd give him just about anything he wanted if he promised to keep smiling at me like that.

"I was thinking I could take you out when you're finished work."

Work. Crap. I glance around the quiet library; for a while there I'd forgotten where I was.

Rhett Jensen is a dangerous creature. He makes me forget where I am, what I'm doing... hell, I think he'd have the power to make me forget my own name.

"Take me out where?" I ask, feeling oddly shy for a woman that sat in his lap on a crowded beach only a few days ago.

I half expected him to ghost me after that day, but I should have known better.

Rhett isn't like any of the men I've known before. He's text me every single day since I last saw him and called me every night.

"Wherever I want," he states with hooded eyes.

I can't refuse him – I could try, but it would be a waste of my time because I'll give in eventually, I know that for certain.

"Okay," I breathe.

***

"If you wanted to drive me home, you could have just asked," I say as I watch the familiar streets pass us by.

He reaches across the centre of his truck and takes my hand before bringing it to his lips and kissing my skin.

He does things like that, touches me so effortlessly and so naturally, it doesn't even give me time to panic anymore. It just feels like something he's done our whole lives.

"Nice try, Lib, but I'm not taking you home."

I pout, but it's nothing more than a habit I've picked up from Ginny. I'm thrilled he's not taking me home. Not yet anyway.

He turns down the street before mine and takes us in a direction I'm yet to venture.

He pulls into a driveway of a big, white house and shuts off the engine.

"Ellie has been asking to meet you," he says casually as he slides from his seat.

I swallow deeply. This is *his* house.

All thoughts of not panicking go out the window.

He's inviting me to his house to hang out with his cat.

I know that's nothing in the scheme of things, but it feels a lot like something a girlfriend does with her boyfriend.

He opens my door when I just sit there, and his brows pull together as his eyes roam over my face.

"You okay?"

I nod stiffly.

"Do you want to come in... or?"

I do, I so badly do, but I'm scared. I'm always scared.

Scared of what's behind me, equally as scared of what's in front of me.

My past, my present, my future.

His fingers skim the bare skin on my arm. "You can trust me, Lib, I'll never do anything to hurt you."

Our eyes meet, and it's the sincerity I see there that has me taking a chance, stepping out of his truck and following him into his house.

He shows me around, never once letting go of my hand, and I'm grateful.

Before I know it, I'm on the couch, a blanket and a cat draped over me and a cup of coffee on the table in front of me.

Rhett sits next to me on the couch, his arm slung around my shoulders and his fingers playing with my hair.

I don't know what I was so afraid of – there's nothing to fear here, nothing except my growing feelings and rising hopes.

Hope is a foolish thing for a woman like me to have.

I know that. I've known it for years, but that doesn't make it any harder to squash down.

Everything is perfect when he's around.

I should know better; perfect and me don't exist in the same sentence.

The niggling feeling in the back of my head that everything is going to come crashing down around me rears its ugly head, and I have to close my eyes for a moment to regain control.

When I open them, Ellie is still on my lap and Rhett is still there, looking at me with a mixture of confusion and intrigue.

He's dying to know what's going on with me.

He's a protector, I feel it, and he's worried that he can't defend me if he doesn't know what I need protecting from.

We've shared so much through text, more than I've shared with anyone. It doesn't feel as personal when he can't see all the things I'm not saying with those perceptive eyes.

"I know there's something you're not telling me."

My heart pounds as I replay each of those words in my mind, over and over and over.

I knew this would happen. That the time would come when he would push me for more, and I wouldn't be able to give it to him.

"Lib, breathe," he commands, leaning in close.

It's only then I realise my breaths are coming out in short, sharp pants.

He cups my face in his hands. "In and out, nice and slow," he instructs, and I comply, my breathing evening out, but my pulse rate spiking for an entirely different reason.

"That's it, baby, breathe."

How can I possibly do something as normal as breathe when he's *so* close?

I press forward, melding my mouth to his.

"*Libby*." He pants as we break apart to suck in a breath of air. "You don't have to hide from me."

I know I can trust him.

I *do* trust him.

That's the problem, trusting him could get him hurt, or worse, killed.

Trust is a dangerous thing for him.

I can't be responsible for anything bad happening to this man.

"Just kiss me," I beg.

He growls, deep in his throat and grabs me, Ellie bolts and I'm in his lap again, just like at the beach, only this time, his restraint is gone and he's devouring me like he's been starved.

His hands slide up my shirt and mine tangle in his hair, pulling him closer.

His lips slide down my jaw, planting kisses on my throat, down to my collarbone and back up to the skin under my ear.

"You're so fucking beautiful, Libby."

I don't care about being beautiful; I just want to be his.

My past has taken so much from me, but I won't let it take him, not yet.

"Make me yours," I whisper.

He stills, the nibbling at my ear stopping as he makes our eyes meet, my golden to his brown.

"You're already mine," he whispers back, his voice hoarse.

Goosebumps form on my skin.

I've never heard something so raw, so passionate... so *true*.

I am *his*, was from the moment I opened my eyes on the bottom of that rescue boat – I just didn't know it yet.

I slide back far enough that I can reach the hem of his t-shirt and slowly lift it over his head, revealing that ridiculously perfect body of his.

My nails skate over his skin and he mutters a curse under his breath.

I love that I can evoke a reaction like that in a man like him. It makes me feel powerful, not at all like the scared little girl I used to be.

"Libby, I don't want to push you... if you're not ready... we can–"

I press a finger to his lips to silence him.

"No more talking."

He opens his mouth to argue, but his rebuttal dies on his tongue when I lift my own shirt over my head.

His hands land on my shoulders and lightly feather down my arms, his wrists brushing the fabric of my bra, it's nothing spectacular – if I'd known when I woke up this morning that I was going to wind up here with him, I'd have put on some nicer underwear.

Rhett doesn't look like he minds; his eyes are taking in every inch of me, greedily and eagerly.

"Are you sure, Lib?" he whispers, his voice pained.

"Do I look unsure?"

He shakes his head.

"I need to be close to you."

That's all the confirmation he needs, his mouth is on mine again, his hands exploring every available inch of me.

He lifts me, my back finding the couch as he hovers above me.

"I had such big plans to sweep you off your feet before we got to this point," he growls.

I think of everything he's already done for me, all the times he's gone out of his way to build my trust... every smile he's saved just for me.

"Consider me well and truly swept," I whisper.

CHAPTER FIFTEEN

Rhett

She tugs at the button on my jeans, and I take the hint, pushing up to my knees as I undo them and slide them down my thighs.

The intensity in her eyes as she watches me causes my dick to harden painfully.

"You know what my first thought was when I opened my eyes after you saved my life?"

Fuck, I hate thinking about that day, but my curiosity demands I know.

"*What*?"

"How gorgeous you were."

I chuckle. "You'd swallowed a lot of water, your head must have been foggy."

She smirks. "And what about now then, huh?"

"What about it?"

"You're perfection, and my head has *never* been clearer."

Fuck I like the sound of that.

I could tell her she's got it all wrong.

She's perfect.

Incredible.

Mine.

But right now, it doesn't matter. All that matters is this moment.

I growl, the feral noise shocking me as our lips meet in a flurry.

I don't know when it happens, but we're both stripped of our clothing and her legs are wrapped around my waist before I can even form another coherent thought.

"I wanted to take my time with you," I rasp.

"Take your time with me later." She moans, breathless as our bodies grind against one another, completely desperate for more.

I nip at her jaw, neck, breasts...

"*Rhett*." Her sweet voice begs me.

"I have to get–"

"If you even think about leaving me here alone to get something as trivial as a condom, I swear to god I'll–"

"Message received."

I've never been this reckless, never not wrapped my shit up, never not even had a discussion about birth control, but with Libby, it's different.

I don't care – I trust her to tell me what I need to know.

I trust her with *anything*, and the idea of her carrying my baby doesn't even scare me in the slightest, so there's nothing to fear.

Not as I push deep inside her.

Not as she moans my name.

Not as both of us find our release.

Not as I fall off the edge of like and into love.

As she looks up at me with those golden eyes that have always held me captive, the one and only fear I have, is losing her.

"Stay with me tonight," I whisper as I kiss the tip of her nose. "I want to sleep next to you."

"I don't really sleep," she replies.

I ignore the flash of panic in her eyes when she realises she's inadvertently revealed something she didn't want to share.

"Lie next to me then. I don't care if we don't sleep, I can think of plenty of other things I'd rather do anyway."

She giggles and blushes, far too coyly for a woman who I'm still buried deep inside of.

"Okay," she whispers.

We get cleaned up, eat some left-over lasagne and then she falls asleep in my arms almost instantly, I decide then that she doesn't know herself as well as she might like to think she does.

***

I idle my truck outside her place and sit on the horn for a few seconds.

I'm itching to lay eyes on her again. It might have been less than four hours since she was in my arms, but it's four hours too many as far as I'm concerned.

Reluctantly as hell, I dropped her off this morning, looking as well rested as I've ever seen her. She's a stunning woman, but I'm not blind to the bags under her eyes or the stress lines on her forehead that are present more often than not.

I glance at my watch again, the minutes ticking over one by one. I toot again.

If she's not out in thirty seconds, I'm going in.

I watch the second hand on my watch like a hawk and I'm just about to undo my belt and climb out to see where the hell she is when her front door swings open and she steps out wearing a yellow dress that makes my heart speed up to a gallop.

I don't know how she does it, but I breathe easier, yet am completely breathless whenever she's near.

She waves out to me and I grin.

My woman is drop-dead fucking gorgeous.

I lower the window on her side and yell out, "Did you get your swimsuit?"

She holds up a bag reluctantly, a frown marring those beautiful features.

I chuckle as she closes the distance from her front door to my truck and climbs in next to me.

Her sweet strawberries and cream scent envelopes me and I let myself drown in it.

I'm craving her something wicked. I crave more of her in every aspect, her body, her mind... I want to see it all.

"You know I hate surprises, where are we going?"

"The beach," I say as I pull away from the curb, locking the doors for good measure, just in case she gets any ideas about escaping.

"Rhett..."

"Just trust me on this, baby, please?"

I glance at her; she's worrying her bottom lip between her teeth.

"Have I ever given you any reason not to trust me?"

"No," she breathes.

"No arguments then."

I steal a few glances at her over the course of the drive. She doesn't say anything and neither do I until we pull up at the beach, further down the stretch of sand than I'd usually swim, away from the prying eyes of my work mates.

"It's like a lake out there," I reassure her.

"Okay."

"I'll be with you the entire time. I promise I'll keep you safe."

"That's what worries me," she mumbles.

"*What*?" I frown, not understanding.

She turns in her seat so she's facing me. "I'm not afraid of the water, I'm a good swimmer."

I take her hand in mine. "Why haven't you been back then?"

She looks up at me with wide eyes. "Because I know you'd do *anything* to protect me, and that makes *you* vulnerable."

"You're worried about *me*?" I balk.

She nods.

I chuckle. "Oh, Lib, you don't need to worry about me."

"Just like you don't worry about me?" she challenges.

I rub at the back of my neck. "That's different."

"How's it different?"

"I don't need you to protect me from anything, Libby. You need me. I can feel it."

She blows out a deep breath – this is heading into territory I know she'll shut down.

She doesn't want to tell me what's going on with her, and I can live with that – for now.

"I don't want anything to happen to you because of me, you've already risked your life once, that's enough, Rhett. I can't stand the thought of anything happening to you." Her voice takes on a hysterical edge, and I'm not sure if we're talking about swimming anymore or not.

"Hey," I soothe, reaching across to tug her against my chest, "nothing is going to happen to me. I'm not going anywhere."

On the outside I appear calm, but on the inside, I'm full of rage, rage at whoever has hurt this woman before I found her.

She's hiding something about her past; Ginny, Cal and I, we all know that, but I don't know what it is... I don't know what she's running from, and that probably means she's right, I am vulnerable because of that, but I don't care.

All I can do is hang in there and hope that one day she'll confide in me.

"I'm not going anywhere."

"You promise?" she whispers.

I pull away and tip her chin so she has to look at me. "Where would I go?"

She shrugs.

"I've got everything I need right here. The beach, the sun, the woman I love, the–"

"*The what*?"

I grin at her. "You heard me, I love you, Libby."

All trace of uncertainty leaves her expression, and she smiles wide. "I love you, too."

I wish I could hear those words every single day.

I wish I could stay in this moment forever.

I wish I could protect her from everything.

I wish I could have seen that nothing is ever easy.

She changes into her swimsuit, and I lead her down the sandy beach to the water's edge.

"After you."

I watch her wade out slowly into the water.

I've never seen anything so fucking beautiful.

I let her get a few feet away before I go after her. She might say she's not afraid, but I don't know how she couldn't be.

I realise in the moment as I reach for her, that she's totally right. I'd put myself on the line again and again for her and that does make her my weakness.

I can't think of a better weakness to have.

I tug her to me, her back to my front as we walk slowly into the calm sea.

Being vulnerable has never felt so good.

CHAPTER SIXTEEN

Libby

"Giiiiirl, don't think I haven't seen you two spending every night together."

Ginny might be a gossip, but she's also not wrong.

Nearly every single night of the past month has been spent with Rhett, all except about five of them.

It's been thirty-one days of bliss.

Breathing easy, sleeping through the night, and then there's the sex. Oh god, the sex.

If there was a choice between sleeping every night and sex with Rhett, I'd happily never sleep a wink again.

The only problem is now that I have him, I can't imagine ever having to give him up, and the reality of my life makes that a very real possibility.

There's been no sign that my old life has followed me here, but I'm not stupid enough to think that it can last forever. It never does.

"Earth to Libby."

I shake my head, snapping from my daydream. "Huh?"

"I said you two should get engaged and we can have one of those ridiculous double weddings."

I snort. "*Right*, because I'm sure that's on Rhett's mind after a month of dating."

"I think you might be surprised by what goes on in that man's mind."

I feel my cheeks heat.

I think I know exactly what goes on in there. He worships every inch of me as though I'm made of pure gold.

"If he asked, you'd say yes."

"He wouldn't ask," I argue.

"*If* he did."

"Then I would *not* say yes."

"*Liar.*"

"You're impossible."

"And you don't fool me."

I'm just about to ask her about the wedding planning and how it's been going when I hear the front door open and close – a sound that prior to meeting Rhett would have filled me with panic, but now makes my heart race for a completely different reason.

I turn in time to see his handsome face smiling as he prowls towards me.

There's no welcome, no greeting, just me in his arms as he kisses me senseless.

"Well hello to you too," Ginny drawls.

Rhett breaks the kiss before going back in, pressing one more sweet kiss to my lips.

I don't think I'll ever get used to the reaction he causes inside my chest. I'm flushed, my breathing is heavy, and my pulse has skyrocketed. All because he kissed me.

He tucks me into his side, his strong arm coming around me. "Oh hey, Gins, didn't see you there," he teases her.

"That's because you were too busy sucking face with my bridesmaid."

"Your *what*?" I gape at her.

"Oh yeah, that's why I came over here, you're my bridesmaid, mmkay? Congratulations on being selected."

My mind races.

Happiness.

Elation.

Fear.

The wedding isn't for another six months.

I could be long gone by then. I *should* be.

It haunts me that I might break Rhett's heart when the time comes for me to move on, but the idea that I could hurt Ginny too is almost too much for me to handle.

This is why I don't usually let people get close to me. I keep my distance, and nobody gets hurt.

People are going to get hurt this time, I can feel it.

My ears ring as Ginny prattles on and on about colour schemes and dress styles. I think I nod and smile in all the right places, but I can't be sure.

Rhett's arms are still wrapped tightly around me and honest to god, if they weren't, I think I would have collapsed to the ground by now.

I love Ginny to death, but I *can't* let her down on her wedding day.

She says something else that goes right over my head then skips out the door with a wave of her hand.

It's not until I hear the door close behind her that Rhett murmurs, "Breathe, baby."

I can't hide anything from him; he *knows*, without me even saying a word, that I'm freaking out.

He's so patient – he fully understands me, even though I'm doing my best to keep him at arm's length.

I feel like I've known him forever.

I try to pull away, but he's not having it, instead keeping me pressed against him.

"Is this about Ginny? Because I can talk to her, tell her all this wedding stuff is too much for you..."

"No," I reply quickly, "I don't want her to be disappointed."

"But...?" he prompts, turning me so we're facing one another.

"But I can't be her bridesmaid."

He concentrates hard, trying to figure me out.

"I don't understand you sometimes, Lib... you love Ginny."

"That's exactly why I can't."

He lets go of me, running his hand through his hair in frustration. "You're not making sense, baby, you're talking in code again."

I *know* I am.

I know I'm not being fair to him.

He deserves the truth.

He deserves someone who could give him so much more than I can.

He strides across the room, pacing out his frustration as I stand stock still, warring with my own head.

I could tell him.

I love this man.

I love him more than anything or anyone else.

He makes my heart feel like it's summer all year round.

He closes the distance between us again and grips my shoulders. "Why does it feel like you're running?" he demands.

Because I am.

Only for once, I'm being pulled in two directions.

For once I have something I want to run towards, as badly as I want to run from my past.

"It feels like you're going to leave me."

He thinks I'm running from him. If only he knew that couldn't be further from the truth.

His eyes plead with me to give him something.

"Marry me," he blurts out, and all thoughts are wiped clean from my mind.

"*What*?" I breathe.

"I heard you and Ginny talking. Marry me, Libby Reed."

I can't believe this is happening; it has to be a joke. It *has* to be. Only, the expression on his face is anything but teasing. He's dead serious.

"I can't," I choke out.

"Why not?" he demands. "I know you feel this. I know you want to trust me. If I have to do something drastic to get you to believe that I'm in *this*, I will. *Marry me*. No more running."

I want to fall into his arms, say yes, go ring shopping and live happily ever after, but I can't give him that. There's only one thing I can give him, and that's the truth. He's earnt it.

"I *can't* marry you."

"*Why*?" his voice cracks, his emotions breaking through.

This is it. The do or die moment. Fight or flight.

"Because my name isn't really Libby Reed."

CHAPTER SEVENTEEN

Rhett

"My real name is Penelope Flórez."

My mind spins out of control as simultaneously, the world around me stops.

Libby Reed – that's the woman in front of me – the woman I'm in love with – but now she's telling me something different.

My mind can't process this.

"Wha– *what*?"

"I was born Penelope, but I haven't been that girl for a long time. I barely even know who she is anymore."

Tears well in her eyes, and I instantly close the gap between us to comfort her – fake name or not, this is still my girl.

My brain is screaming at me to get answers, to find out why she's lied to me all this time, but my heart... all that cares about is making her feel safe.

I feel her tears soaking through my shirt as she cries, and I just hold her, bearing some of the weight, because I know deep down that she's carrying something much too heavy for her shoulders.

She's got a secret that could destroy everything I thought I knew about her, but I want to know it anyway. I *have* to know.

I kiss her head, her hair, her cheeks.

She eventually calms down and tugs herself free.

"We should sit," she says as she swipes at her tear-stained face.

I nod in agreement and lead her to the couch, making sure not to put any distance between us.

She's still mine, she still needs *me,* and I won't believe otherwise until she tells me herself.

"I'm scared," she finally says after several long moments of silence.

She's not the only one.

"I'm scared too, but it's like a band aid, just rip it off quick and it'll hurt less."

She takes a deep, calming breath, then starts talking. "I'm in the witness protection programme."

Well fuck. That is the absolute last thing I expected to come out of her mouth, but as soon as it does, it all makes sense. *Everything.*

The looking over her shoulder.

The not sleeping.

The panic about the TV cameras.

The reluctance to get close to anyone.

I fall back against the couch, totally lost for words. My head is whirring with questions, but I can't voice any of them.

"*Why?*" I manage to choke out.

"Because I gave the authorities everything they needed to convict my father," she shudders, "Antonio Flórez."

Jesus.

Sweet baby Jesus, *no.*

"*Antonio Flórez* is your father?"

"You know who he is?" she whispers.

Everyone knows who he is. Big time mobster. Absolute scum of the earth kind of dude.

Her father.

I don't know how the fuck something so perfect came from something so vile.

"It was all over the news when he got sentenced and sent to prison," I explain, "I remember the name."

I wrack my brain trying to come up with the details, but it was such a long time ago, years even, so I don't recall much.

"How long have you been hiding?"

"Four and a half years."

Jesus.

I turn to her, taking her hands in mine. "He's behind bars, baby, *for life*, right? He can't hurt you."

She almost laughs, the defeated sound bursting from her. "He knows it was me, Rhett. *He* might be behind bars, but he has plenty of people who aren't. They're looking for me. They're *always* looking for me."

Fucking hell.

"So you just keep running?"

She nods, a tear slipping slowly down her cheek.

"I haven't spent more than six months in one place since he went to jail. Marco doesn't give up, and he's calling the shots now."

"Marco?"

Her faces pales, and her voice goes quiet. "He's my dad's right-hand man. But honestly, he's even worse than my father because he's not afraid to get his hands dirty."

"Can't the police do something? Throw him in jail too?"

"If they could find him, maybe... maybe not," she whispers. "You don't understand that world, Rhett, he's like a ghost. Laws, rules... they barely exist where I come from. Men like Marco, they do what they want – take what they want, whenever they want it. Me included."

Fucking hell. I can't deal with this. I want to hunt down and kill the bastards that hurt her. I want to see their blood on my hands.

I tug her into my arms; I need her close before I lose my mind.

"I really do love you; you know?" she says through her tears. "That part was never a lie."

Fuck, she's breaking my heart. The shit she's been through, I can't even comprehend. My life is simple compared to hers.

"I know, baby," I soothe, "I know you do, and you know what?"

She pulls back enough to see my face. "*What*?"

"I love you, too."

She sniffs. "Even though I lied to you?"

"You didn't lie to me, you protected yourself, there's a difference."

"It feels like I lied."

"Look at me," I demand when she tries to hide her face, "you're still my sweet, beautiful, Libby, okay? You're *mine* and nothing you say could change that."

"Nothing?"

"*Nothing.*"

"Not even if I told you I was forced into marrying Marco?"

Marrying Marco... she's married?

She's married and it's not to me.

It hurts, it hurts like a knife to the gut. Knocks the breath clean out of me.

This poor fucking girl.

I pull her close and kiss the top of her head, reassuring her as best I can. "Not even that."

"Rhett, you can't say that, I'm *married*. I'm married to a monster. Have been since the day I turned eighteen."

I grip her face in my hands and press a kiss to her lips. "You aren't married to anyone, baby, *Penelope* is. You're Libby now, and you won't be wearing any man's ring."

"Not even yours?" she whispers as she snuggles into my chest.

That makes me smile, even in amongst all this bullshit. "I've asked the question, Lib, all you have to do is say the word."

***

It's late when she stirs in my arms. She fell asleep not long after confessing everything to me.

I would have slept with her, but every time I closed my eyes, visions of that news report came flooding back to me.

After a few hours, I got my cell phone out and googled her father's name. I had to know what he was convicted of.

The answer made me shiver.

Human trafficking, drug distribution, underage prostitution, murder... the list went on.

I don't know how much of that life she had to live but, given that she was married off to a mobster boss's side kick, I assume it was a fair fucking bit.

She breathes out heavily as I stroke her hair gently.

I don't know how she did it, but she got out – she survived.

Not only that, but she helped take her father down.

That might have led her to me, but at what cost?

I'm not an idiot, I know the size of the target on her back right now. You don't put a man like Antonio Flórez away for life and walk away without consequences, not when his crew is still walking free.

She's faced all of that, on her own, for over four years.

I stare down at the woman in my arms.

I've always thought of her as fragile, but now I see how wrong I was. She's the strongest person I've ever met.

"Rhett?" she asks, her voice sleepy.

"I'm right here," I reply, tightening my arms around her.

We're still on the couch. I thought about carrying her up to bed, but I didn't want to risk waking her. She needs all the rest she can get; just living day to day must take it out of her.

"I fell asleep?"

I kiss the top of her head. "You went out like a light."

She snuggles in closer again. "You know that's because of you."

"Me?"

"I only sleep when you're with me."

"Well then you should know I'm all too happy to offer my services, any night you want."

"You mean that?" she breathes. "You really aren't going to run a mile?"

It's almost comical that she's worried about me running, when *I'm* the one who should be scared about *her* bolting at any second.

"Where would I go?" I ask her again, the same question from the beach, right before I told her I loved her.

Everything else might have changed, but that simple fact has remained the same.

I love her.

I love her more than I ever thought it was possible to love another person.

I love her so much, that if she *does* run, I know damn well it's going to destroy me.

She looks up at me, every emotion under the sun swimming in her eyes.

The soft glow of the TV casts a shadow across her face, and she looks so perfect, my breath gets caught in my throat.

"I love you," she breathes.

"I love you more."

"Impossible," she murmurs as her lips find mine, searching softly for permission.

I hate the unease she's experiencing about my feelings towards her. She owns me, *completely*; her father being a bad man isn't going to change that.

Some bullshit legal document saying she's married isn't going to change that either.

She left that life behind; hopefully she won't do the same to me.

"I can practically hear your thoughts whirring," she whispers.

"It's a lot to take in," I admit.

"I'm sorry."

She dips her head, but I stop her, catching her chin between my fingers. "Don't you dare apologise."

"I'm going to have to leave one day, you understand that, right?"

I don't understand it at all, I mean, I do, but I don't like it. Not one bit. As far as I'm concerned, it's not happening, she's not leaving, not without me.

"Then I'll go with you."

Her eyes widen. "You can't just give up your life and follow me on the run."

"I can do whatever I want, Libby, and what I want, is to be with *you*. I'll do whatever it takes to help put you back together, *anything*, and I'm going to fuse little pieces of myself in every crack so it's impossible for you to leave without taking me too."

"*Rhett...*"

"Don't," I interrupt her, "don't worry about something that doesn't matter, *not yet*. They haven't found you here and they probably never will. You're safe with me, Lib. Anyone wants to cross you, they'll have to get through me first."

"You getting hurt is my biggest fear," she confesses.

"And losing you is mine."

CHAPTER EIGHTEEN

Libby

I've got new locks on every window, new deadbolts on all my doors and enough security lights to keep the place lit up like a Christmas tree, all night long.

I'm not sure if it's for their peace of mind, or mine, but I'm grateful for it nonetheless.

Rhett suggested that I talk to Ginny and Cal about my situation, and I'm glad I listened to him and let them in on my secret. They've been nothing but supportive, if not a little over the top.

They don't know everything Rhett knows, like the fact that I'm legally married, but they know enough to explain why I'm such a head case, and that's a relief.

I know I'm breaking all the rules, being in witness protection is like fight club, and everyone knows the first rule of fight club, but I've been alone a long time, and I don't want to be alone anymore.

Breaking my silence technically puts me at more risk of being found, but I trust these people, I love them, and it seems like they love me too.

I've finally found a place in the world where I want to belong.

Rhett pauses in the doorway, catching my eye. He winks at me and my stomach flutters as I watch his fine ass walk inside.

He's carrying a box for some elaborate-looking camera system that I flat out refused, and he went ahead and bought it regardless.

He and Cal have been arguing for the past half an hour about where the best placement for the cameras are.

I don't even know why they're bothering setting it up here; Rhett has had me staying at his house every night anyway, so if that thing has to go up somewhere, it may as well be at his place, but I doubt there's a chance in hell that I'll get away with that suggestion.

"Just put it up and stop bickering like old women," Ginny snaps when they start up again. She rolls her eyes at me. "Those two are impossible. That system will never get installed and I'll never get my bestie back."

I giggle. "I'm just around the corner at Rhett's."

"Exactly." She pouts. "You're all the way down there and not right next door where you should be."

"Don't blame me, I didn't even want the stupid cameras."

Cameras aren't going to protect me; they're just going to show me what's coming for me.

"Well it was three against one, so suck it up," she announces brightly.

I don't bother arguing, it'll just be another argument I won't win.

"You and Cal are going to need to get new black-out blinds so you can sleep at night." I wince as one of the guys tests out the latest security light.

Planes flying overhead are going to think it's a freaking landing strip.

"Then we'll get black-out blinds," she replies, sassily.

I roll my eyes. "This is all a bit of an overkill, don't you think? I stay with Rhett every night, or he stays with me, he drives me to and from work pretty much every day… if I'm not with him, I'm with you. I don't know when you guys think I'm going to get hurt, I'm never alone."

"Save the spiel for someone you've got a chance of cracking, sweetheart." Cal chuckles as he comes back outside and heads down the steps.

He's right. I'm wasting my time. Ginny doesn't negotiate.

We watch as he jumps the fence between the two properties and jogs out back towards his shed.

"Thank god, now I can put these damn things where they *should* be." Rhett appears behind me and my entire body hums with awareness.

My eyes track him as he reaches up, a slice of that perfect abdomen visible as he tests out the positioning of one of the cameras.

He pulls out a drill, and even though I know the cameras are a waste of time, I can't help but appreciate how good he looks putting them up.

Ginny swipes at my chin with her finger, interrupting my ogling.

"You just had a little bit of drool."

"Shut up." I giggle, swatting her hand away.

Rhett's eyes find mine, and he smiles wide. God, I love it when he smiles at me like that.

I can never remember how many wonders of the world there are these days, but Rhett smiling should be added to the list.

"Jokes aside, girl," Ginny says as Rhett goes back to his work, "that man looks at you like you hung the moon."

"He asked me to marry him."

"I'm sorry, he *what*?" she demands, tugging me further around the porch so we're out of earshot.

"Not like on one knee with a ring or anything. Not like Cal did it." I nibble on my bottom lip. "I don't even think he was serious. It was just before I told him about... *everything*... he said he thought he needed to do something grand to gain my trust."

"And he went with a marriage proposal?"

"Apparently."

"What did you say?"

I shrug. "I told him everything."

"No," she swats my shoulder, "not *that*, what did you say about getting married?"

"He wasn't serious, Gins."

She peers around the side of the building. "He looks pretty serious about you from where I'm sitting."

I follow suit and look at my man, working hard to keep me safe.

He loves me, I can see that. I can *feel* it. He's putting me back together, piece by piece and that only makes me more scared.

The time will come when I *have* to leave. It always does.

He's said he'll go with me, but he doesn't know what he's saying. Being with me could mean giving up who he is, quite literally his whole life.

I'm due to check in with my case worker next week and I've got this bad feeling in the pit of my stomach.

I was at work yesterday when Asher, one of the other librarians, told me that a man had been asking for me.

I don't know if I'll ever stop feeling that sense of complete and utter panic when something like that happens.

It was just one of my regulars, looking for a book I recommended the week before, but my pulse raced for the rest of the day – right up until the moment Rhett walked in the door.

I shouldn't rely on him this much, but I do. I can't help it, every time I need something, he's right there, offering it before I've even asked.

He's showing me that good men are still out there, and well and truly stealing my heart in the process.

He really is my hero.

***

"I've got to check in with my case worker," I blurt out the statement, as though saying it fast will make it any less scary.

I don't know why I get myself so worked up about it, the police know roughly where I am, they gave me this name, they advised me to come to this town... if they needed to tell me something urgently, they could find me fast enough, but calling in to talk to Malcolm still makes my hands shake every single time.

I hate the unknown.

"What for?" Rhett questions, the hand holding the seasoning above the pot on the cooktop pausing as he arches a brow at me.

"I have to call in once a month."

"There's nothing you're not telling me, right? You look nervous."

I shake my head. "It's just routine… and I *am* nervous. I never know what they're going to say."

He sits down the small jar and gestures for me to come to him. I do and feel more settled instantly. He has such a calming effect on me.

"I'm sure everything is fine. No news is good news, surely?"

"Usually," I whisper.

I've got a bad feeling. I always have a bad feeling, but this is different. I feel like I'm on borrowed time now that I have something – *someone* – here that I don't want to run from.

"I'm scared they're going to tell me to move on," I admit.

"We'll cross that bridge when we come to it, Lib." He presses a kiss to the top of my head, and I melt.

I love that he still calls me Lib, even now that he knows it's not my name. I think I'll always be Libby to him, and I'm grateful for that. This is the closest thing I've ever had to a clean slate.

"But I mean what I said," he carries on, "I'll go with you, anywhere you are is where I want to be."

It's the sweetest gesture I've ever received, yet it's firmly in the top ten things that are *not* happening. I can't ask him to do that. Not for me.

"I'm sure it'll be fine," I murmur.

"Why don't you call in right now and then we can eat without you worrying yourself sick?"

I nod in agreement and slide my phone from my jeans pocket. I hit dial on Malcolm's number and wait for it to ring out.

I've changed my number since we last spoke, so he answers with a generic, "Malcolm Tim speaking."

"This is Libby Reed," I reply.

I never give him my real name. Other than telling Rhett, I haven't spoken the name *Penelope* since I fled my home nearly five years ago.

"*Libby*," he says, his voice carrying that same relieved tone it always does when he hears from me.

I like Malcolm. He's a decent man. He's older, with salt and pepper hair and a kind smile.

I wouldn't say I trust him with my life in the way I do Rhett, but for a long time now I've had no choice but to follow his lead anyway, and I'm still here, alive and well, so he must have been doing something right.

"Everything okay on your end?" he questions.

"Everything is fine."

"I tried to call you a few days ago, but as expected, the line was dead."

My heart thuds against my rib cage.

Calm down. I tell myself. Him trying to reach me isn't a good sign, but he also didn't send a patrol car out to find me, so maybe it isn't too bad.

"What is it?" I whisper, turning away from Rhett as his eyes pierce into mine.

"I don't want you to panic." I almost laugh. No sentence that starts that way ever ends well. "... but Marco Adelmo is back above ground."

My breath leaves me in a rush. I'm excited, and that probably makes me naive.

"That's a good thing, right? You can arrest him?" I squeak.

I don't want to let myself get too enthusiastic, but this could be *it*, without Marco running shit, it'd all fall apart. Sure, my father will still want me to pay, but there's no one else in his crew that cares enough to go to the lengths that Marco has.

If Marco were gone, I could have my freedom back. I could have a real life.

"We brought him in... we couldn't charge him with anything, I'm so sorry."

Just like that, all my hopes disappear.

I should have known better. He's too smart. He's too good at being bad.

He's already five hundred steps ahead of these cops; he always is.

If he's above ground, strutting around, parading his freedom – then he's probably planning something. Whether or not that something concerns me is anybody's guess, but if there's one thing I know about Marco, it's that he holds a long grudge.

"What do I do now?" I whisper.

"That's entirely up to you, but I recommend that you move on – put yet another steppingstone between you and him."

"Move on?" I repeat, my voice hollow.

"We could have you a new identity in less than twenty-four hours."

I hear Rhett drop something, and I spin around.

He curses under his breath before abandoning the mess and rushing to me.

"Is someone with you?" Malcolm asks, surprise colouring his tone.

"Yes...things have changed for me."

"Changed *how*?"

"I met someone. He knows everything."

I feel a weird tremor as Rhett wraps his arms around me, and it's only once I look at my hand that I realise I'm the one shaking. My whole body is vibrating.

Malcolm blows out a breath. "I'm happy for you, Libby, I really am, but I can't lie to you and say that this doesn't complicate matters."

Tears start running down my face, and my lip trembles.

I don't know what to say, I'm already aware of just how complicated things are now.

Rhett holds his hand out for the phone, and I pass it over. I'm in no shape to converse right now anyway.

"This is Rhett Jensen, I'm here with Libby, she's feeling a bit overwhelmed."

I can't hear Malcolm, so I just cling to my lifeline and listen to his voice.

"I'm her boyfriend."

I hug him tighter.

"Is there anything to suggest that Marco knows where she is?"

He's silent as he listens.

"Right, okay, so there's no reason for her to leave."

Another few beats of quiet.

"I know that, but I assure you she's safe here. We've put precautions in place."

I *feel* safe here.

"*I* can protect her."

He already does.

"With all due respect, she can't run forever."

He's right. I *can't*. I don't have it in me.

I take a deep breath, do my best to get my shit together and remind myself that I didn't come this far just to break down now.

This is just another day I need to be strong.

I hold my hand out for my cell and Rhett passes it over but catches my hand before I can speak to Malcolm.

"Don't you want a life, Lib? A real life, one with a husband, a family? Maybe even a dog?"

I want those things. I want them so badly. I never thought they were on the cards for me, but when I look at him, I hope that they are.

"He's smart, Rhett, you don't know how smart he is."

"Then let's stay strong together. Two is better than one."

He's right. I'm stronger with Rhett at my side, we're better together.

I know what I need to do, no matter how much danger it might put me in.

"Malcolm, listen… I've made a decision. I'm staying. If there's no immediate threat, then I'm not going to run and hide. If Marco is where you can watch him, then that works in our favour, right? He can't touch me if he's nowhere near me."

Malcolm sighs again. I'm sure the stress of this job must take its toll on him.

"I understand your decision, and between you and me, I think it's about time you found someone to share this burden, but professionally, I have to advise you that this isn't the recommended choice."

I look up into Rhett's brown eyes and I know I'm doing the right thing.

"I understand that, but I'm staying anyway."

CHAPTER NINETEEN

Rhett

"If I asked you an honest question, would you give me an honest answer?"

She peeks up from her book and glances at me curiously. It's been days since she spoke to her case manager, and honestly, I've been sitting on this question since the minute she hung up the phone to him, trying to find the right time to ask it.

"I think so." She smirks.

I pat the space next to me and she crawls up to occupy it after setting her latest novel down.

The girl damn near reads a book per day. I've given up trying to keep up with which book she's got her nose stuck in.

I seek out her skin, my fingers lightly skimming up her arm as she presses her body against mine.

I can't keep my hands off her.

I love the way I can make her shiver all over, or shimmy when tingles race up her spine.

"So, what's this big question?" she asks, her hands settling on my chest, her honey-toned hair spilling on the bed around us.

"I want to know about your tattoo."

That thing has been taunting me ever since the day I first saw it.

I've laid eyes on it hundreds of times between now and then, and I know that Libby doesn't like it being seen... the only question is *why,* and I can't wait any longer to find out the answer.

She stills, her breath catching, before she exhales. "But that's not a question."

"Will you tell me about your tattoo?" I try again.

She smiles, a small, sad smile.

"You got it when you were sixteen?" I press.

She shakes her head.

"No?"

"Fourteen," she whispers. "I lied."

Who the fuck gets a tattoo at fourteen years old?

"A mobster's daughter," she replies, answering a question I wasn't aware I'd asked out loud.

"He made you get it?" I choke out.

"*All* the girls had to get them."

Jesus Christ.

I know some of what she's been through, but honestly, I think I've been too scared to ask about other aspects of her life before witness protection. I know my limits and I'm reaching them already – I don't know what happens when she tells me something that I can't handle, but I'm worried I'm about to find out.

I swallow deeply, my fingers running up and down her skin in a steady rhythm to help calm me. "*All the girls*?"

She swallows slowly, choosing her words.

"You know what kind of man my father is, the things he did..."

On the inside I'm in a fit of rage, but on the outside, I have to stay composed – try to anyway, for *her*, but if she answers this next question with anything other than the word 'no', I'm going to lose my mind.

"Libby, were you... did he–"

"No." She cuts me off before I even get the question out. "No one ever touched me."

Thank god for that.

I would have taken on the world to end him if he'd let that happen to her.

"No one would have dared. I was earmarked to be Marco's since I was eleven years old. I got my brand when I was fourteen."

I physically shudder at her casual use of the word 'brand'.

The way she said 'to be Marco's' makes me want to hurl, then want to kill the man she was forced to marry, right alongside the man who fathered her.

"What is it... the tattoo I mean, what does it represent?"

"All the other girls got a tattoo that incorporated an 'A' and an 'F', to show that my father owned them."

"And yours?"

"Mine has an 'M' and 'A'... to show that Marco owned me."

I've never paid a lot of attention to the circular design at the base of her spine, right above her ass, but right now I wish I'd looked harder. Another man's initials make up that image, and they're marking the skin of *my* woman.

"He's never going to own you again, Lib."

She looks up at me, and I don't miss the look of fear in her eyes. "You promise?"

It's foolish of me to promise something that relies so heavily on the actions of another person, but I need her to know that I won't back down, not from a mobster, not from *anyone*.

"I promise, he won't touch you as long as I'm breathing."

Her eyes glass over. "Don't. Don't talk about yourself like that. I couldn't live with myself if something happened to you because of me."

"And I couldn't live with myself if something happened to you, period."

She spends a long moment just searching my eyes, saying so much without saying anything at all to me.

She doesn't need to. I know exactly how she feels. We'd each die trying to protect the other.

We're each other's strength, whilst simultaneously being each other's biggest weakness.

"Lib, I have to know... about Marco. Did he hurt you?"

"He never got the chance," she breathes. "I got away on our wedding day. I was never given the opportunity to run before, so I took the first one I got."

"You make it sound like you never got to leave the house?"

She shrugs a delicate shoulder. "We didn't have a house, we had a guarded compound, and I barely got to leave that either. I could go weeks without seeing other people. I mean, there were the other girls, but they went as fast as they came, and I wasn't allowed near them often, my father was worried they'd corrupt me."

She laughs humourlessly.

What a sick joke. As if anyone could ever corrupt her more than her dear old dad.

"Libby, *fuck*... I can't even imagine."

"Don't try to," she begs. "It's not something I want you to try and live."

"Where's your mother?"

Her eyes fill with tears. "She was barely a teenager when she had me. He picked her out because he liked her eyes – that's what he told me when I was eight – she died giving birth to me. He didn't get her the help she needed."

Fucking hell. I feel tears in my own eyes. It's too much. She's been through too much to still be this strong.

"I don't know anything else about her, but maybe it's better that way..."

I hold her close as she breathes through the pain that is her past life.

I refuse to acknowledge it as her life, because it's gone now – it's over and she's never going back.

"How'd you get through it, baby, how'd you come from that and turn into you?"

She's so smart, so *normal*. I don't know how she did it.

"Books," she answers simply. "They gave me a normal that my life couldn't – they taught me everything I know. I figured out pretty quickly that the life I was living wasn't a normal one. Hookers and gangsters, drugs and murder... I knew I had to get out, I think I was about ten when I realised what a bad man my father was. It was a long eight years from that point on."

Jesus. My woman, she's smart, strong and beautiful.

She had to sit in that hell hole, for nearly two decades until she got a chance to escape.

I kiss the top of her head. "You're here with me now, Lib, *safe*. And nothing is going to change that."

"I really hope you're right."

"I'm right, trust me."

She slides her hand down my side, her fingers teasing their way down to the waistband of my pants, her eyes hooded and seductive.

I'm a smart man, I know where this is heading.

That's when it occurs to me. She ran out on her 'wedding night', she's been in hiding ever since...

"Lib, please tell me I wasn't your first?" Her hand stills and I reach for it, urging it on – begging her to continue. I don't want her to stop. Not for anything in the world.

She obliges, her fingers teasing me as she shakes her head softly. "I went through a... *stage*, back in the early days on the run. I drank a lot, went out all the time... and one night there was this sweet guy with kind eyes... I guess I just wanted to feel close to someone."

She looks up at me with regret, and I shake my head at her, I don't want her to feel remorse for something like that, the one-night stand is every young person's right.

"Was he good to you?"

"He was, but I never saw him again after, it was just once, and honestly, it was pretty fumbled and awkward."

I chuckle. "Sounds about right."

She slides her hand into my jeans, and I hiss as she wraps her palm around my dick that has been hardening with every second of her torturous descent.

"He had nothing on you," she practically purrs, and I let my head fall back in pleasure as she strokes me.

She stops, sliding her hand out and reaching for the hem of her shirt to pull it over her head as she straddles me.

"You kill me, Libby. You're so fucking beautiful."

My hands find her hips, holding her in place so I can look at every inch of her absolute perfection.

"You own me," she whispers.

Those three simple words hit me like a wrecking ball and embed their way under my skin and into my veins until she's flowing through my entire body.

She's been owned, literally and figuratively in her past, yet here she is, ready and willing to be owned again – albeit in a far healthier way – by *me*.

I sit up so we're pressed together.

A moment passes and her bra is on the floor.

Another moment and my clothes are gone, my shirt, my pants, followed by hers. They all join the pile next to the bed until we're stripped bare to one another, and when I slide inside her, I thank the powers that be, that she found her way here, to me.

CHAPTER TWENTY

I grin like an idiot as I read Rhett's note again.

I know I'm probably owed some good karma, but I still have to pinch myself every day to make sure I'm not dreaming – that a man like that, loves a broken woman like me.

He's never lied to me, he's never put me in harm's way – he does everything with my best intentions at heart, and that's something I could get used to.

He had the early shift at work this morning, so it's a rare day that he won't be driving me to the library.

I really need to learn how to adult better and get myself a license and a car. I bet Rhett would teach me if I asked him.

I honestly think he'd do just about *anything* for me.

I grab my bag and let myself out the front door to start the walk to work. I tuck the note into the side pocket of my bag so I can read it again later on my break.

Who needs romance books when you've got a boyfriend as sweet as mine?

I wave out to Ginny, who's in her front window, still in her pyjamas.

I don't know how that woman does it. Just last week I saw her doing a video conference at her dining table, she had a blouse on, and under the table, she wasn't even wearing pants, I swear she'd just rolled out of bed and she still rocked that thing like the absolute boss bitch she is.

She waves back vigorously and spills her coffee down her front in the process.

I'm still giggling half a block later.

I'm laughing right up until I spot a silver sedan with tinted-out windows slow down and pull up to a stop just ahead of me.

The engine stays running, the car idling at the curb, and just like that, I'm transported right back to a time when my every move was watched. I barely went anywhere in the first eighteen years of my life, but when I did, it was always with an escort who made his presence known.

I divert my path down a side street to avoid walking past the car. I know I'm being paranoid. Marco would never drive a car like that, he's a huge, SUV kind of guy and the only colour on his radar is black – like his soul, he certainly wouldn't have plates on his vehicle like the ones I just memorised out of habit.

All that doesn't make the knot in the pit of my stomach ease at all, though.

I consider calling Rhett, but I know him too well, if he thinks I'm in danger, or even that I'm just feeling out of my comfort zone, he'll drop everything and come to me – it's just the kind of man he is.

I can't call him every time I get nervous. If I'm going to do this, if I'm going to stay in one place and not run, then I'm going to have to learn to relax.

I glance back over my shoulder and to my relief, there's no sign of the car, but just in case, I decide to stop at the small convenience store at the end of the street.

Seeing other people might help me to get some much-needed chill back.

I duck inside, the welcoming smile of the familiar man behind the counter instantly putting me at ease.

No one is going to attack me, full stop, but if they were, they're certainly not going to do it in here, surrounded my Mr. Wright's five hundred security cameras.

I give him a wave and stroll the aisles as I let my breathing even out.

I wander down another small aisle, crouching to grab a tube of toothpaste. I'm standing back up when the tampons catch my eye and I grab a box of those too.

I carry on around the shop, collecting a couple more items as I go.

I glance at my watch, the last thing I need is to be late for work, but I've still got plenty of time.

My thoughts wander to Rhett and what we got up to this morning. I blush at just the thought of it.

He mentioned that it was his last condom and given that I plan to see him again tonight, that's an issue.

I double back until I find something I never in a million years thought I'd be buying.

I glance around to make sure no one is around and grab the biggest box I can see off the shelf.

I rush to the counter, stacking the items in a pile for Mr. Wright.

I feel like my face is going to burst into flames. I'm so embarrassed, like everyone on the entire block is staring at me and the box of condoms that scream, 'look at me, I have a lot of sex'.

Mr. Wright doesn't even bat an eyelid as he rings up my total and I pay.

I stuff everything into my bag and rush out of the store like it's on fire.

I was panicking about one thing when I walked in, and now I'm almost giddy with awkwardness from my first ever experience buying protection.

I might have seen a lot more in my life than most people, but I sure as hell haven't ever felt more like a teenager than I just did.

I'm almost pleased with myself.

I decide to cut through a park to speed up the trip, and I'm about halfway across when it starts to rain, making people scatter – run for shelter and pull out their umbrellas.

I hear my phone ringing in my bag, but I can't get it out yet, it'll get soaked. I hope it's Rhett, I'm dying to tell him how mortified I was buying a box of rubbers. He'll laugh his head off – probably tell me how sweet I am.

I've got my umbrella out of my bag and I'm putting it up in front of me when I bang into someone, my phone going with a shrill ring once again.

"Oh my gosh, I'm so sorry," I say as I lift my umbrella to see who I've run into.

I haven't even laid eyes on him when I know.

His scent gets me before anything else does; I'd know that smell anywhere.

My eyes meet the electric blue ones that have plagued my dreams for so many years and a single word falls from my lips.

"*No.*"

My knees just about give out from underneath me as I hear the words that confirm my worst nightmare has become my reality.

"Hello, Penelope. Long time, no see."

***

I'm numb as he shoves me into the waiting, blacked-out SUV.

I was right about his taste in cars, I think to myself.

I haven't cried, haven't screamed.

There would be no point.

No one would come, and even if they did, Marco will kill them. I don't need any more blood on my hands.

Marco slides in next to me and the car pulls away from the curb before he even has the door shut.

Only two men. Maybe I have a chance.

I almost laugh at my own stupidity. There's no way it's just the two of them – not yet anyway.

There will be more vehicles, more men, more power.

That's Marco's style; he's more of a 'build an army' kind of man. There is no way he came out here vulnerable.

My phone starts ringing again, and my thoughts go straight to Rhett. I hope like hell that Marco doesn't know about him, because if he does, then he'll be the next to die. Right after me.

I already know I'm dead. This is the end for me; it's only a matter of time.

You don't hide from a guy like Marco and not suffer the consequences.

You don't put Antonio Flórez behind bars and not give your life in return.

It was easy to believe that things could be different when I was with Rhett. He made everything better, he made me think I could have a life like that, but he was wrong. My past always comes back to haunt me.

"How'd you find me?" I ask, my voice sounding bolder and braver than I feel.

Marco is silent, and I know he's waiting for me to look at him before he speaks. I might have been away a long time, but I haven't forgotten how things work.

I give him what he wants, meeting his stare with all the confidence I can manage.

If he's going to kill me, I want him to see that I'm not that scared little girl anymore. I'm not his meek wife.

He studies me carefully, his handsome face in deep concentration.

He's so quick that I don't even see it coming before he backhands me across the face.

It's so hard that I feel my brain rattle in my skull and my teeth feel like they're going to fall out of my mouth.

The pain is so intense, but I know it's nothing in the scheme of what he's capable of. It's nothing compared to what he'll do to me before he ends my life.

I cover my face with my hand, blinking back the yellow spots blurring my vision.

We're still driving, racing down the streets far too fast, the heavy rain pelting the windscreen.

"Give me your phone."

The moment of light-headedness passes, and it occurs to me that my phone is ringing yet again.

I can't seem to get the message to my hands that they need to move, and when I sit there like a deer in the headlights, Marco snatches my bag from my lap and tips the contents over the seat.

He snags the phone, holding up the screen for me to see that it's a private number. It's called me eight times now, and I don't have to guess who it is.

Malcolm.

He'll be warning me. Warning me about what has already happened.

As much as it pains me to know the desperation he'll be feeling, being hours away, and knowing that danger is coming for me, I'm so glad that it's his name on the screen and not Rhett's.

"The police are at your house," Marco drawls, "as if I'd be stupid enough to take you there."

I don't ask how he knows that. He knows *everything*.

He will have men everywhere; they've probably been watching my every move since I left the house this morning, maybe even longer.

I don't reply.

He grazes his eyes over the rest of the contents and my heart sinks when he reaches for the box of condoms, bringing them up to his face. "You know, I always told your father we should have put you out with the other whores. Seems like you're good at opening your legs."

Another tear slips free and I resist the urge to swipe it away. He's like a wild animal, unrestrained and unpredictable, and the same rules apply here as they would in the wild – no sudden movements.

"I bet that little boyfriend of yours likes you acting like a whore."

I gasp and he chuckles.

"What? You thought I didn't know about him?" he reaches across the space, his fingers caressing my cheek. "I know everything, Penelope. I've had men watching you for weeks... you're mine, *remember*?"

My skin crawls with repulsion and bile burns in my throat.

If he's been watching me for weeks, then he knows about everything. Rhett, Ginny, Calum... everything.

For the first time since I laid eyes on him, I'm glad that he got me alone. Maybe once I'm dead, he'll leave them alive.

I just hope however he's going to do this, that he at least makes it quick.

"You want to know how I found you?"

I nod, one short bob of my head.

"You're famous, Penny, didn't you know?" His voice is harsh, filled with malice and mocking.

"I don't know what you're talking about," I whisper.

He grips my chin tight, hurting me. "I saw you on a news website, you stupid bitch. You could have just drowned; it would have saved me the hassle."

My shoulders sag, the wind knocked clean out of me.

I should have left.

That very day, I should have run.

I knew nothing good would come of that camera, but like an idiot, I stayed. I hoped for more and it came back to bite me in the ass.

If I'd left then, I wouldn't be here now. About to die.

But then I wouldn't have Rhett.

I close my eyes, Rhett and his beautiful smile filling my mind.

Marco might be able to take my life, but he can't take my memories. I find some comfort in that as we turn off towards the marina.

I know I should scream or try to throw myself from the car or something, but I've lost any and all fight. It would be pointless, even if by some miracle I made it out of the car, I'd never get away.

All I want to do is pretend that I'm at home with Rhett, that his fingers are touching my skin, that his mouth is on mine... his deep brown eyes looking at me with more love than I could ever possibly deserve.

The car pulls to a stop, but Marco doesn't move.

"I wonder if lover boy thinks he'll be able to save you this time?"

My blood runs cold as I slowly peel my lids open.

I know I shouldn't say a word – that the only right answer here is my silence, but I can't sit back and say nothing, not when it's *his* life on the line.

"Leave him out of this."

He chuckles darkly. "But you make it too easy, *mia*."

I wince at the use of the name both he and my father used for me when I was younger.

I look at the man in front of me; he's charming, gorgeous and alluring, if this was another life – if he was a different man – he'd be considered a catch, but he's dark – darker than I thought possible. Darker than any man I've ever met, bar one.

I almost feel sorry for him, the way he was groomed by my father from such a young age, but then I remember that I was raised the same way, and I never, *ever* would have let that darkness win.

"Get out of the car," he demands. "Let's give your little boyfriend a call."

CHAPTER TWENTY-ONE

Rhett

I duck inside and pull the door shut behind me, tossing the soaking-wet rain jacket in the corner of the room as I go.

I don't know what the hell would possess anyone to want to be out in this type of weather, let alone swimming at the beach in it, but I guess some people just like the thrill.

The huge sets rolling in off the ocean are no joke right now, not something to be taken lightly. They could pull me in and swallow me whole and I'm a much better swimmer than most.

I shake the water out of my hair as the door swings open again, the wind howling as Nick fights to get it closed behind him.

"Got those signs secured, boss."

"Good man." I nod at him.

We've officially closed the beach. It's not something that happens often, but with the harsh, sudden and unexpected storm that just rolled in, we had no choice.

"Can you keep an eye out on the sand, I sent that group of teenagers on their way, but something tells me that listening might not be their strong suit."

"You got it."

He heads up stairs to the watch tower and I'm about to shoot over to see if Georgie has everything sorted in the equipment shed, when I hear my phone ringing from my bag.

I glance at my watch, and *shit*, I forgot to check in with Lib. She was going to call me when she got to work safely. She should have been there over an hour ago and I've left her hanging.

I curse under my breath as I rummage through my bag for my cell.

Her name is on the screen when I pull it out, and I hit answer, apologising as soon as I get the phone to my mouth. "Hey, baby, I'm so sorry, it's crazy down here with the storm."

"Rhett!" I hear her scream, but she's in the distance.

I can hear wind, rain and her sobs and in that same moment I can feel my fear threatening to bring me to my knees.

I don't want to think the worst, but I can't help it, my mind is already there.

They've found her. She's been taken.

"Libby?" I yell, my feet in action even though my whole body feels numb, taking me across the room towards where Becca is.

"*Libby* isn't here right now," a deep, male voice snarls, and any hope I had of my girl being safe and sound is dashed.

"Where the fuck have you taken her?"

Becca turns, mid-sentence, her words lost on her lips as she takes in the look on my face.

The voice, the one I assume belongs to Marco, just chuckles arrogantly.

"Call the police," I mouth to her and she rushes past me, over to where the phones are.

"You know, all this could have been avoided, if she'd just known her place."

"She knows her place, it's here with me," I reply.

I grab a sheet of paper and scrawl down the words, 'police' and 'get Malcolm Tim'.

Becca nods, the phone already at her ear and ringing.

"That's funny, because from where I'm standing, she's right here, with *me*."

Think, my brain demands of me. *Listen.*

I quickly catalogue what I know.

Libby has been taken by Marco.

He's likely somewhere within the area, because there hasn't been enough time for him to go further with her.

She's scared and alone.

The promise I made her flies through my mind and I'm overcome with guilt. I couldn't protect her. I should have been there. I should have kept her safe.

"All out of demands, lover boy?" he taunts me, and my brain clicks into gear.

I can feel guilty later, right now all I need to do is think, do what I can to help Libby.

I listen hard, there's not much to be heard over the wind and the rain, but there's something there, a sound that's familiar, but one I can't place.

"Let her go, come after me instead," I plead.

He just laughs. "Try and save her this time, *hero*."

Fuck. No.

"Say goodbye, *mía*."

"Lib!" I scream down the phone.

"Don't come for me!" she yells before the line goes dead.

***

Becca thrusts the phone at me before I even get the chance to take a breath.

"Hello?" I bark.

"Rhett, this is Malcolm – Libby's case manager, have you spoken to her?"

"She's been taken," I choke out.

He's silent for a beat before launching into action. "Who did you speak to?"

"I assume it was Marco. I thought you were watching him? How the fuck did you let this happen?"

"An error in judgement," he explains, regret thick in his tone, "the last time we saw Marco Adelmo was yesterday morning. We had no way of knowing that he knew her whereabouts, as of only two hours ago we've raided his warehouse and found evidence that suggests otherwise."

I try to swallow the lump lodged in my throat. "What evidence?"

"Photographs, videos... it looks as though he had his men collecting intel on her for weeks, maybe even months."

"Jesus Christ. We were meant to keep her safe!" I yell, slamming my hand down on the desk top.

"I'm aware of that, Mr. Jensen, and trust me, if we can't get her back, then I'll carry this with me for the rest of my life, but now isn't the time, I need you to think, I need you to give me anything you can. I've got local police checking her house and tracking where her cell phone is, but Marco is a smart man, he's not going to be caught easily."

"He didn't tell me anything." I rake my hand over my face and glance one by one at my work mates who have gathered around, each of their faces a pale mask of fear.

None of them know Libby's situation, but they've never seen me like this. I'm cool under pressure, composed. I don't yell. I don't panic. But it's different when it's the woman I love.

Everything is different.

"What did you hear?" he urges.

"Wind, rain..." I close my eyes, trying to replay it in my mind. "Water," I say slowly. "I heard water, sloshing... like it was hitting a dock."

"Anything else?"

"The hum of an engine."

Just like the one I used to let lull me to sleep after my dad and I had a long day fishing.

"He taunted me about saving her," I whisper as it all clicks into place.

He's at the dock.

"He's getting on a boat. He's going to drown her."

I'm out the door, sprinting towards my truck, not even bothering to hang up the call.

There's no time.

I have to get to Libby.

I don't know what the hell I'm going to do once I get there, but I have to do *something*.

My cell rings as I try to see through the heaving rain pelting my windscreen. I don't even recall bringing it with me, but there it is.

I hit answer on the blocked number. "Libby?" I yell.

"It's Malcolm," he replies.

I should have known it wouldn't be her. Her name wasn't on the screen, but my mind isn't working right. I'm frantic.

"Where are you headed, kid?"

"To the marina, it's not far from here, I might be able to stop them."

"I have a team dispatched as we speak, Rhett, I need you to stand down."

I growl, deep in my throat as I get closer and closer to where I need to be. "If you think for even one god damn second that I'm staying behind on this, then you must be fucking high."

There's silence for so long that I think the line must have been cut off, so when he finally speaks, it surprises me. "Alright then."

CHAPTER TWENTY-TWO

Libby

The boat lurches up over the giant swell and my stomach rolls.

It's an insignificant thing to be worrying about, but I really hope I don't puke.

The rain is relentlessly pelting down on me as I huddle in the corner of the boat that Marco threw me in.

He's standing over me, the dark grey sky behind him.

"It didn't have to be like this, mía, we could have had everything," he yells over the noise of the weather, engine, and the raging sea.

He's right. We could have had everything, but at what cost?

The world is a better place for having my father locked up, and now that Marco is going to kill me, all I can hope is that they catch him and put him away for it too.

The empire will crumble with the two of them out of the picture. I've seen how loyalties fail when the boss is away. Marco took over effortlessly, because he's smart – he's too smart for this life that he's chosen.

The world would probably already be rid of everything my father built if it wasn't for the man standing before me.

He turns his back on me when I don't answer, and I take the opportunity to tug some strands of hair from my head and wedge them down into a join in the boat's interior. If I'm going down, then I'm going to do my best to ensure he's going down too.

I'm about to scratch myself enough to draw blood, so I can leave some behind, when the boat slows and the guy driving turns to face Marco and I see his face for the first time.

I recognise him – he's worked for my father forever. He's not much older than I am. I remember him from when we were younger. I used to follow him around the compound and beg him to hang out with me.

Andre.

Even though he's probably here to help kill me, seeing him makes me sad. He's just another example of the lives my father corrupted.

He must have really stepped up to be allowed to be the only person out here while Marco gets this job done. Only his most trusted are privy to seeing murder first-hand – only the people he trusts won't *ever* talk.

"How's this?" Andre yells over the noise.

Marco makes a show of looking around dramatically, as if he can even see anything with the rain and driving winds.

"Looks like the perfect spot to drown a snitch," he replies, malice in his eyes as he glares at me.

"Better a snitch than a murderer," I throw back.

I figure if this is it, *this* is the end of my life, then I may as well go down saying what I think – showing him who I am now.

Rhett taught me that some things are worth fighting for and that my life is one of those things.

"Want me to shut her up?" Andre offers, holding up a roll of duct tape and taking a step in my direction.

Marco waves him off. "Let her talk, she won't be doing it much longer."

Andre chuckles and moves back to the driver's seat, where he kills the engine.

The boat rocks violently and I pray for a rogue wave to come and take me overboard. It'd be a kinder way to die than whatever hell Marco is going to put me through before he offers me to the sea.

"Just get it over with already."

Marco crouches down in front of me. "But where's the fun in that, *mía*."

His hand trails down my cheek, sweeps across my neck and down to the neckline of my shirt.

I feel sick to my stomach and this time it's got nothing to do with the motion of the boat.

"I never did get that wedding night, Penelope, maybe we should rectify that right here and now."

I feel tears springing in the corners of my eyes, and I'm grateful for the rain in that moment – at least he won't see me cry while he abuses me.

He roughly grabs at my top, tearing it in half.

I try to move back, but I'm trapped in the corner – there's nowhere to run.

He chuckles at the fear in my eyes. "What's the matter? A whore like you should have no problem spreading her legs."

"I'm *not* a whore."

He gets right in my face then, and the fear I've had for him up until this moment is nothing compared to the dread I feel in the pit of my stomach now.

He's going to kill me, but first he's going to make me beg for death.

"Be a good little wife and get flat on your back."

I shake my head, tears spilling down my face, mixing with the rain and the splashes of saltwater.

He sneers and before I can register what he's doing, I'm on my back, soaked from the water pooling in the bottom of the boat, my jaw aching from where he's struck me. He's tugging at my jeans, undoing the button and lowering the zip.

"No," I sob, over and over again, "no, no, no, god *no*."

He's got my hands pinned above my head, and no matter how much I struggle, he's too big, too strong... I'm no match for him.

I force myself to fight as he hovers over me, struggling one-handed to move the fabric of my jeans because of how soaking wet my legs are.

I'm drenched from head to toe.

I buck my hips in an attempt to throw him off, but the sick bastard likes it. He likes my struggle.

"Rhett," I sob into the cold air. I know he can't hear me, but just saying his name aloud makes me feel closer to him.

"He can't save you now, bitch."

He's looking at me with those evil, beautiful eyes and I can't take it anymore. I roll my head to the side, about to give up and shut down entirely when my gaze lands on Andre; he's moving towards us, a crowbar raised high above his head.

I open my mouth to scream, but he shakes his head and holds up a finger to his lips.

I don't understand. I don't want to believe that he could be on my side... that he might be able to save me.

My heart thumps in my chest as he creeps closer, preparing himself to swing.

I wince upon the impact, Marco's heavy body landing on me, all his weight pressing into mine.

I shove at him, trying desperately to get free as Andre drags him off me.

A harsh breath leaves me before being sucked back in, deep into my lungs, chilling me to the bone.

I try to get up, but I trip, my jeans around my thighs hindering me. I shiver as the cold wind blows through my ripped shirt.

"It's okay." Andre looks at me frantically, his eyes raking over my exposed body. "I won't hurt you."

I try to get my jeans up, but it's a struggle, I'm numb with cold and fear.

"Whh- why?" I stammer, my teeth chattering.

I don't understand. He's here with Marco – Marco trusts him, and Andre just betrayed him.

"I've been undercover since I was seventeen."

I can't believe this. My eyes dart to Marco, his limp body lying lifeless in the corner of the boat.

"I was arrested when I was sixteen; I had enough drugs on me to kill a horse. Instead of throwing me in prison, I was offered a deal. Take down Antonio Flórez. Once you put your father behind bars and ran, my position was made redundant... so they changed my focus. I was there to gather intel on Marco and to help you if the situation ever arose."

"All those years," I breathe, "because of me."

He nods solemnly. "Because of *me*. But it's better than life behind bars for being a drug runner, right?"

I'm not sure I agree with that entirely, but at least he had some freedom out here I guess, either way, I'm so grateful.

"I can't believe this," I whisper. "You saved me."

"And now you're both dead." A snarl comes from behind Andre, and I look just in time to see Marco tackle him, the pair of them tumbling overboard.

The boat rocks violently, sending me flying, and I stumble into the water after them, hitting my head as I go.

CHAPTER TWENTY-THREE

Rhett

The huge police boat powers through the rough sea like a wrecking ball, leaving a white trail of water in our wake.

"I've got a location," one of the cops yells to the one behind the wheel.

I don't know who these guys are; they don't look like the local police around town, but from the minute they turned up, they've run like a well-oiled machine.

The only reason I was allowed aboard this thing was because Malcolm called ahead and gave authority. Not that five guys in uniform could have stopped me anyway, not when it comes to Libby.

He barks out a bunch of coordinates and we make a sharp right turn, heading further out to sea.

"How do you know where they are?" I demand.

One of the guys looks at me, then to the man who must be his superior, who nods.

"We've got a man on the inside. He switched his GPS tracking device on a moment ago," he explains.

"You've got a guy on the inside, and she *still* got fucking taken?" I yell.

"It's not all black and white. If he couldn't get that tracker on until now, there's a god damn reason for it," he replies, less than impressed with my accusation.

Well he can get fucked. I couldn't be less impressed if I tried.

My girl is out there, scared and alone, and if she's not still breathing by the time I find her, then I'm going to bring a fresh hell to the lives of the men responsible.

"There." The one behind the wheel points, and in the distance, through the huge swells and the sleeting rain, I see the small boat, rocking.

"I can't see anyone on board."

I grab a pair of binoculars like the ones the man next to me is looking through, and after some difficulty, I manage to locate the boat. The *empty* boat.

"*No*," I whisper, as I move my search to the water, scanning the area around the vacant boat.

"I see something," I yell as I find splashing in the water. "A person."

The boat lurches forward, speeding faster, and I drop the binoculars to rush to the side of the boat as we get closer and closer.

"I've got eyes on two," someone yells.

Two. One of those *has* to be her.

Please, let her be okay.

"Two males," another voice confirms.

"No!" I roar. "Libby! Where are you?"

I can't see any sign of her anywhere. We stop and all I can see is two men, each desperately trying to force the other under the water.

"Get in there," I demand to anyone who will listen.

"Stand back, sir, we need to survey the area, we're not able to enter the water until that's complete," one of them tells me.

Fuck that. Fuck all of this.

I step away and rush to the other side of the boat, throwing myself overboard into the out-of-control sea.

I hear yelling behind me, but I don't give a shit, I'm not going to sit back and wait while these assholes make their assessments about the two in the water.

Those men are *nothing* to me. Libby is *everything* and she's out here somewhere.

I swim as hard as I can, my arms cutting through the water faster than I thought I was capable of until I reach the smaller boat.

I drag myself up the back, my calf smacking into the motor painfully as I lose my balance.

"Libby!" I scream again, but there's still no reply.

I see three men enter the water from the police boat, but they're heading for the struggle.

I scan the water, and that's when I see it. It's not much, but the flash of white is enough.

"Over there," I yell, pointing, before I throw myself back into the water.

Every stroke of my arms, every gasp of air, her name is on repeat in my head like a mantra.

Libby, Libby, Libby.

I just have to get to her.

I eat up the distance between us in a matter of seconds, and then she's in my arms, her lifeless back pressed against my front. There's blood running down her face and her eyes are shut.

I tread water desperately as I shake her, trying to get a response. "Come on, baby," I beg. "Wake up."

I hear the boat's engine nearby. "Somebody help me!" I scream.

Somebody help her.

I tap her face, her chest, but there's *nothing*.

My vision blurs, from the exertion or from tears, I have no idea, but her name is still on repeat, from my lips this time, begging her to come back to me.

I hear voices, feel arms pulling and I jerk away, no one can take her from me.

"Rhett, give her to me, let me help her," someone says. "Let me help Libby."

The voice saying her name pulls at me, gives me the strength I need to see what's in front of me.

The boat is right there, and three men are reaching for Libby to pull her on board.

I push forward, the surge knocking me against the tin exterior as they pull her to safety.

I scramble after her, another set of arms helping me up.

"Let me help," I croak, desperately shrugging off hands to get to her.

"We've got her," I'm told as I drop to my knees next to the body of the woman I love. "Let us do our job."

Her clothes are torn, her skin bruised and bleeding.

She's a complete mess, and I'm so fucking in love with her.

I watch as she's checked over, the boat already in motion, and when I hear the words, "she's breathing," a wrecked sob escapes me.

She's alive.

"Looks like she hit her head pretty bad, we're going to need to get her straight to the hospital, but I think she's going to be just fine."

A hand claps down on my shoulder. "You're reckless as hell, man, but you did it. You saved her."

I can't take my eyes off her as her chest delicately rises and falls with each breath.

She still hasn't opened her eyes, but she's *alive*, she's here, and I was only just in time. That piece of shit nearly ended her life.

If he's not already dead, I'll kill him myself, witness cops be damned.

"Where is he?" I demand through gritted teeth. "Where's the fucker that hurt her?"

"Dead," a shaky voice from my left says.

He sounds the way I feel. Beaten, *broken*. It's intriguing enough for me to pull my eyes from my girl to see who's spoken.

He's soaking wet, mid-twenties if I had to guess. He's obviously the inside man, and as much as I'd like to punch him in the face for not getting help sooner, I need to know that the scum that took my girl is no longer breathing first.

"You sure?"

"Killed him with my bare hands," he replies.

Well, that might *just* be enough to stop him getting his head smacked in.

"I'm going to pretend I didn't hear that, Andre," a cop says as he wraps a blanket around my shoulders.

"*Rhett*?" I hear my name, a raspy, barely-there whisper, but I hear it. I'd hear her voice anywhere.

"I'm here, Lib," I reply as I shuffle forward, resting my forehead against hers. "I'm here, you're going to be okay."

"Marco–"

"Is gone," I finish for her. "He's never going to lay a finger on you again."

"Andre?" she asks, her lids finally lifting enough for me to see her stunning golden eyes.

"He's right here, Lib, he's going to be just fine as well."

She lets out a pained, relieved sob, and I vow that I'm never going to hear that heartbroken noise from her sweet mouth again.

I'll show her that I can protect her, even if it takes me the rest of my days.

I want to be at her side for the rest of my life.

I want to keep her safe, sleep next to her and wake up with her every single day.

I've never been as scared in my life as I was these past few hours, and I know one thing for certain, I never want to be without her, *ever again*.

So there's only one thing I can ask of her in this moment.

"Marry me, Libby?"

She blinks once, her mouth slowly curving up. "I can't think of a single reason why not."

***

"You can go in and see her now." The nurse smiles at me as she emerges from Libby's room. "But I want you to promise that you'll see a doctor once you're done."

"You drive a hard bargain."

She laughs but points her finger at me in warning. "I mean it, Mr. Jensen, if I come back in an hour and you still haven't seen a doctor, I'll be dragging you there myself."

"Yes, ma'am." I nod.

She shakes her head, still grinning, as she mutters something about me being a stubborn fool.

I limp into Libby's room, my leg screaming in protest. The doctor is still in here with her, her chart in his hands.

And there's my girl.

"*Lib*." I breathe easily for the first time since they wheeled her away from me. "Are you okay?"

"She'll be just fine with some rest," the doctor reassures me.

I hobble to her side, desperate to be as close to her as possible.

She clasps my hands in hers, the bruising and stiches on her face doing nothing to dull her beauty.

"I was so scared, baby," I admit as I drop into the seat near her head.

"I was scared too." Her eyes gloss over with tears.

I turn back to the doctor. "Are you sure everything's okay? Her head?"

"We've done a CT and it's come back clear. All I can prescribe right now is time to heal and rest."

"I think we can handle that."

"Everything looks great with your blood work too, Libby, but we'll be monitoring your pregnancy very carefully over the next few weeks – your body has been through a trauma and–"

"My *what*?" Libby gasps at the same time as I say, "sorry, what?"

He frowns, his eyes moving between Libby and me. "I'm not quite sure what the question is?"

"My pr–*pregnancy*?"

"Yes..."

"Doc, this is the first we're hearing about any pregnancy," I blurt out.

His eyes widen in surprise and his mouth makes a small 'o'. "Well then I guess I should be saying congratulations. You're about ten weeks along. I'm so sorry, I assumed that you'd informed the nurses, it's noted here on your chart with your blood results."

I can't speak. My brain can't make the words form.

Pregnant? A baby? Us?

"That's *impossible*. I had my period last month, right on schedule, I'm due again any day."

"I'm afraid that's not overly uncommon, a lot of woman experience what they believe to be a period during early pregnancy. You might find that you won't bleed at all this month, your HCG levels are nice and high."

Libby opens her mouth and shuts it several times without saying anything.

I know how she feels.

My brain was pretty much maxed out when I walked into this room and now it's on overload.

"I've got the ultrasound technician on her way down now to check that everything is okay with the baby, so I guess it's lucky I spilled the beans now rather than when she was scanning your uterus."

"Do you think... the baby... what if it's hurt?" Libby stammers, concern written all over her face.

I grip her hands tighter, fear for the child I didn't even know about coursing through me.

That baby, planned or not, is a part of her, a part of me. It's so unbelievably wanted in only the thirty seconds since I found out about it, that the idea of it being hurt threatens to tear me in two.

"There's no reason that the baby won't be absolutely perfect. You weren't struck in the stomach, and you've not been drugged, so I'm sure it's all looking great."

His pager beeps and he glances at it before excusing himself from the room, leaving us both reeling.

"We're having a baby?" I breathe.

"We're having a baby," she confirms, tears running down her face.

I've got her wrapped in my arms in a second, gently tugging her close. "Lib, what's wrong? You don't want a baby?"

She splutters out a laugh. "I couldn't want a baby more."

I pull back to search her face. "Then what is it?"

"I'm so happy," she sobs, causing me to laugh.

"Oh, sweetheart." I chuckle. "God, I love you."

"I love you, too."

"We're going to be a family."

I can barely believe the words coming out of my mouth. When my relationship with Kelsey ended, I never could have imagined that it would be the best thing that ever happened to me.

"I never thought I'd get one of those," Libby whispers.

Her life before never would have allowed for a real family, not a healthy one, but that's not her life anymore. Her life is here. With me.

Marco is dead and Andre gave the police everything they need to make arrests on anyone left with any power.

The threat isn't gone, but it's been reduced to the point where I won't lose any sleep over it. Libby is safe.

"You've got one, Lib, you've got me. Forever," I promise.

EPILOGUE

Rhett

"I can't believe I'm doing this. This is no way for a married man who's about to become a father to behave."

She rolls her eyes at me. "Nice try, babe, but I'm not giving you an out from this one."

I chuckle, my futile attempt at escaping, failing. "*Please?*"

"No can do I'm afraid." She grins.

I don't even know why I'm wasting my time.

I lost fair and square.

When that woman came into the lifeguard tower and offered to donate a percentage of the profits of her calendar to our organisation, she wasn't playing fair. She knew we wouldn't say no to having more money to help us save lives.

Nick, Blake and I drew straws, and guess who lost?

It *had* to be me.

Cal and Ginny have been riding me about this ever since I told them, and Libby hasn't been much better if I'm honest.

You'd think she'd have a problem with me getting my gear off in front of a camera, but no, apparently, she's only all too happy for me to oblige. I think she's even been asking how much to buy one of the damn things for home.

"We're nearly ready for you, Rhett," Jane, the woman in charge calls to me from down the beach.

I wave at her and she turns back to her photographer.

"I can't believe this," I mutter.

Libby smirks. "We'll just be over here cheering for you." She rubs her growing belly and giggles. "Go daddy... get your gear off."

I rest my hand on top of hers as I chuckle again.

I don't know how the hell I got so lucky. I scored myself the perfect woman.

We got married two months ago, just the two of us with Calum and Ginny there to witness us making our vows.

We could have waited until after the baby, and had the whole wedding, white dress and all that, but neither of us cared about making a big show. I just wanted to be able to call her my wife.

And now I can.

And what a wife she is.

"Sorry," Jane interrupts, "but I was just brainstorming some ideas for your tag line."

"My tag line?"

"Yeah, I've got things like *The bad-boy mechanic, The cocky pro-surfer*... I was thinking 'The *something* hero', what do you think?"

I shake my head furiously. "I'm not a hero."

"He's the biggest hero I know," Libby tells her, "I think it's very fitting."

I groan. "Seriously, I appreciate the compliment, I really do, but I'm no hero, I'm just out here doing my job like everyone else."

Jane grins, like I've somehow given her a great idea.

"*The humble hero,*" she announces, "it's perfect."

"Oh, I like that," Lib agrees.

"He's not *that* humble," Cal's voice chimes in from behind me, "in fact, I'd say he's overconfident."

I rake my hand over my face before turning to face my best mate. "What the hell are you doing here?" I grumble.

He chuckles, Ginny joining him in laughter. "Did you really think I was going to miss this? I've been waiting years to see you pose in a speedo."

"That's incredibly weird." I grimace.

"We brought popcorn," Ginny announces proudly.

"Oh *god*," I breathe.

"Chop, chop, muscles, day's a wastin'," Cal taunts me as he sits down next to Libby.

I shake my head. "I'll remember this, you all know that, right? I'm great at holding a grudge."

"You hold that grudge, dude, it's no skin off my nose," Cal says as he grabs a huge handful of popcorn, because oh no, they weren't joking about that.

Jane laughs as I kiss Libby on the cheek and get to my feet.

It's for a good cause, I remind myself. *Good cause, good cause, good cause.*

"Screw it. Let's just get this thing done." I tug my shirt over my head and throw it playfully at Libby.

I strut down the beach, a chorus of wolf whistles and cheers behind me.

OTHER TITLES

Love like Yours Series
Rushed – Book 1
Pierced – Book 2
Hunted – Book 3
Chased – Book 4

Rock Games Novels
Paper, Scissors, Rock: Vol. 1
Hide and Seek: Vol. 2

My Heart Duet
My Heart Needs
My Heart Wants

Calendar Boys Novels
Mr. January
Mr. February
Mr. March
Mr. April
Mr. May
Mr. June
Mr. July
Mr. August
Mr. September

Mr. October
Mr. November

ACKNOWLEDGEMENTS

The songs that inspired this book: *Take On The World* – You Me At Six, *Have A Little Faith In Me* – John Hiatt, and *Wanted* – Hunter Hayes.

I can't believe this is the second to last book! To everyone reading, thanks for hanging around eleven books later, and those who won't read this until after December because you're binge reading them all, I hope you're enjoying them!

Libby and Rhett stole a little piece of my heart, and I hope they hold a place in yours too.

Thanks, as always, to my editors, BETA's, street team and the crew in my reader group – I see you, I appreciate you, I'm so grateful for all the support!

See you in December!

ABOUT THE AUTHOR

NICOLE S. GOODIN is a romance author and mother of two from Taranaki in the North Island of New Zealand.

In mid-2015, she started to write about a group of characters who wouldn't get out of her head. Her first book, Rushed, was published in mid-2016.

Nicole enjoys long walks on the beach, pillow fights and braiding her friends' hair. She dislikes clichés, talking about herself in the third person, and people who don't understand her sense of humour.

Please feel free to contact her either via her website, email, Instagram, Twitter or on her Facebook page, she would love to hear your feedback. If you're feeling really game, you can even sign up for her newsletter.

Visit www.nicolegoodinauthor.com for more information.

UPCOMING TITLES

Calendar Boys Novels

Mr. December

9 780995 127654